That Boy Ain't Write in the Head

By
Paul K. Metheney

Edited by Karen T. Newman

Copyright © 2021 Left Hand Publishers, LLC
5753 Hwy 85 North #6092 Crestview, FL 32536
All rights reserved. ISBN: 978-1-949241-27-3

https://LeftHandPublishers.com
Twitter.com/LeftHandPublish
Facebook.com/LeftHandPublishers
editor@LeftHandPublishers.com
Cover design by Paul K. Metheney

Acknowledgments
Special thanks go out to Karen T. Newman, and her company, Newmanuscripts.net, for her tireless efforts in editing.

Recognition should also go out to our friends and families who tolerated our working hours during the creation of this publication.

To the readers who purchased this volume, thank you.

CONTENTS

Foreign and Domestic
A Secret Service agent must attack the President

L MINUS FIFTEEN DAYS

"We don't want you to spy on the President."

"Good, because that's not going to happen," Special Agent Robert Jackson says to the man stumbling beside him, without looking at him.

"Could we jes' stop running for a danged minute? I ain't jogged this much since the Bush administration."

"Yes, sir," Jackson replies, looking at his watch. He continues to run in place.

"Really? Do you have to keep doing that?"

"I have to keep my heart rate up. This is not for my health. It's for his."

The older man bends at the waist, wheezing to catch his breath.

As he jogs in place, Jackson inhales cold, crisp snap of spring air in D.C. The cherry blossoms will be coming soon, though for now, the air has enough edge to require a jacket. It's too early for a noxious fog of automobile exhaust to contaminate the chill.

Earlier, Jackson spotted him ahead on the mall sidewalk, obviously intent on intercepting the special agent, while pretending to stretch in preparation for a pre-dawn run. Jackson continues to jog toward him, casually unzipping his hoodie for easier access to his shoulder holster if need be. Trying to look nonchalant, his uninvited running mate begins to trot slow enough so Jackson will effortlessly catch up to him. As he approaches, Jackson automatically sizes him up. Older, impatient, although not nervous, unarmed, no martial arts training, no situational awareness, brand new track suit, out of shape. No danger. In the split second his subconscious mind evaluates a threat level, Jackson's consciousness recognizes White House Chief of Staff, Richard Monteath. Monteath gamely tries to run alongside Jackson as he puts forth his proposal, hands to his ribs, begs for a stop.

"Agent, we know you are good friends with POTUS and have been for a while."

"I have been on the President's protection detail since before his first presidential campaign, back when he was a senator," says Jackson, legs still pumping in place.

"You're more than that. You're his lone friend. His confidant. The man has isolated himself from everyone, including the First Lady. You're the only one he truly talks to anymore." Monteath's gasping has settled into quiet wheezing.

"What specifically is it you want from me, sir? I have less than forty-eight minutes to finish my run, shower, dress, and report for duty. How can I help you?"

"We honestly ain't sure, son," Monteath says. "And by 'we, 'I mean the whole danged country. We need you to keep your ears open. Listen to President McAllister. Let us know if there is anything to worry about. In case you missed it, he ain't precisely been acting hisself lately."

"No, sir."

"Is that 'No sir, he ain't been hisself or 'No, sir, I won't do it'?" Monteath asks.

"No, sir, I won't do it."

"What?" Chief of Staff Monteath is not accustomed to hearing "no."

"No, sir, under no circumstances, will I spy on the President of the United States of America," Jackson says politely. "If one of my protectees does not believe they can trust me, I lose effectiveness in being able to do my job. Effectiveness in my job is a difference between life and death. In this particular case, the life and death of the most powerful man in the world."

"Now hold on a minute, son. We don't want you to spy on nobody," Monteath backpedals. "We want you to keep an ear out in case POTUS does or says anything to embarrass the office. If you haven't noticed, he ain't precisely running with all his wheels on the rails these days."

"And as you may have noticed, President McAllister is not exactly an idiot. Sir." Jackson says, teeth clenched, "Even if I were willing to betray my position, my protectee, my service, and my oath, do you honestly think a Nobel Peace Prize winner and Rhodes Scholar won't notice if someone is spying on him?"

"Agent Jackson, like you said, he is the most powerful man in the world and he needs his friends looking out after him and right now he thinks of you as his one friend. We don't need you to spy on POTUS, we sort of need you to look out after him ... and maybe stop him if he tries to do something to embarrass himself, the office, or the country."

"Sir, if I were to look out for him as you suggest, how long do you think he might consider me a friend?"

"Well, son, what's more important? What President McAllister thinks of you or the welfare of your country?" Monteath asks, one eyebrow raised.

"Mr. Monteath, when I joined the Secret Service, and even before that, when I joined the Marines, I took an oath to protect America and its Constitution from enemies both foreign and domestic. What you are describing is a 'coup d'etat.'" Jackson stops jogging in place and faces the Chief of Staff. "And it's 'Special Agent Jackson.' Not son."

Jackson turns and sprints toward Pennsylvania Avenue.

*

"Good morning, Mr. Jackson, so nice of you to join us," the head of the White House security team comments from podium. It would be like any other college classroom, if all the students were federal agents wearing nondescript suits, SIG Sauer P229s, Motorola XTS radios, and surveillance kits. Aside from the security chief, Jackson, at thirty-four, is the oldest of the President's detail. Similar briefings are convening in identical rooms in the building for the First Lady's detail, as well as the Vice President's.

"Sorry. COS Monteath detained me," Jackson explains.

"Anything you would care to share with the group?"

"No, sir. Not at this time."

"Okay then. As we were about to wrap up," the security chief looks pointedly at him as Jackson takes a seat at a desk, "there are no new threats on the board. 'Osprey' is in the nest for the rest of the week and advance teams are securing upcoming travel. Night shift reports no incidences with a single exception of Osprey walking the halls a bit last shift. Keep your comms on and do a great job. Get out of here."

Secret Service agents filter out as Jackson approaches the podium. His detail chief hands him a briefing folder. "The COS, Jackson, really? Before six a.m.? What'd he do? Climb in the shower with you?"

"Close. Tried to run with me in an *accidental* meeting."

"Oh man. Richard Monteath tried to keep up with you? I would have paid good money to see that," his chief says. "What'd he want?"

"I think he wants me to spy on the President," Jackson whispers.

4

"Shit. Did he say that? Exactly? The words 'spy on POTUS'?" The Secret Service chief's head reels with the implications of what his special agent is telling him.

"Not exactly. He wants me to 'look out for him.' You know, Osprey," Jackson says.

"Okay. That's different. Technically, 'looking out for him' is the essence of your job. No harm, no foul. Did he happen to mention why he wanted you to do it? You're not gunning for my job, are you, kiddo?" the security head smiles.

"Wouldn't have it if they gave it to me. You take all the criticism, we just intercept the bullets. I'll stick with the bullets. He talked as if I were the President's BFF and alluded to the idea he thinks Osprey is losing his shit. He made it sound like he wants me to report any info directly to him."

The head of White House security rubs his chin for a moment.

"Well, you don't work for him. You work for me and I work for Treasury, so until they do give you my desk, do your job like you always have. Screw them and their games. You keep Osprey safe and we all get to collect a retirement check."

"Roger dat."

"That conversation does tie in to an email I got, though," the security head says. "Last night, Monteath's office called HR and had your jacket pulled. Because of who we look out for, HR BCC'd me a copy of your file they sent over. Somebody on Pennsylvania Avenue wants to know all there is to know about you. Looks like it might be Richard Monteath himself. Do you want me to talk to his office? You want me to shoot him? I will. I've got a gun. Somewhere."

"Nah. We've probably heard the last of it. I played the coup d'etat card on him and then walked away," Jackson says.

"Alrighty then. Keep me in the loop." The security chief puts all his files in an attaché case. "And next time you feel like accusing the White House Chief of Staff of treason, could you give me a few days' notice to put in for vacation?"

*

"What have you done now to embarrass me?" First Lady McAllister asked.

"Darlin', I have no clue about what you're yappin 'about."

"Don't 'aw, shucs 'me, David," the President's wife hisses. "We've been married too long. I absolutely know when you are lying and definitely when you have done something idiotic or thinking about doing something idiotic. Which is it?"

"Darlin', I honestly have no idea what you are goin' on about. I have been having some strange dreams lately. Got to do with a desert trip we took years ago."

"What? Oh, no. Not that. I have put such silliness out of my head. You should too. Merely a trick of light or something," she says.

"Weren't no trick of light. I talked with those folks and I'm telling you they was as real as you are standing there with your hands on your hips."

"Well, you better never tell that story to anyone. We've worked too hard to get here and I ... I mean, WE have plenty to do before we're out of here."

"Don't you worry your pretty little chemically colored head about it, honey. I think I figured what I need to do. And I need to do it quick."

"David," the First Lady says, "if you embarrass me, I will make you rue the day you ever met me."

"You're about two decades too late there, honey-bunch."

*

L MINUS TWELVE DAYS

"Bob, could you come in here for a few minutes?"

"Yes, sir." Jackson relays his stepping into the Oval for a few minutes into his wrist mic. Before he moves, a nearly identical suit takes his place outside the veranda door to the office.

"How can I help you, sir?"

6

"Nothing urgent. I wanted to chat a bit. Sit down, would you?" President McAllister asks.

"We're not supposed to, sir. It would be best if I stand," Jackson says.

"Dammit, Bob, I am your Commander in Chief, don't make me get a platoon of Marines in here to jam your ass into one of them butt-ugly Queen Anne chairs."

"Yes, sir, if you think that would do it."

The President smirks as he sits in the chair across from him, legs crossed, coffee cup in hand. "Would you like something to drink?"

"No, thank you, sir."

"Smart man. The coffee sucks here. How can you screw up coffee?"

"One would think it hard to do, sir," Jackson replied.

"Well, never underestimate the power of the U.S. government. Anyway, did I ever tell you about the time the First Lady and I got lost in the desert? This was before she was the First Lady. Hell, before I was even a senator."

"I don't believe you did, sir."

"We were driving along, lost as all get out, she was bitching up a storm, and I decided to pull over into this gas station. Out in the middle of nowhere. She thought it was to ask for directions.

"While she was in the ladies' room, I go in the station and look at every little thing in there. I buy a candy bar, an orange Nehi. You ever had an orange Nehi, Bob? Right out of the cooler, ice-cold. Not a damned thing better in this world. I buy her a bottle of water, the First Lady doesn't believe in sodie-pop. I look at a map for a different state. I pay for some gas and generally dilly dally for about twenty minutes.

"I come out and pump the gas all while she is madder than a snake in a hot bucket. It's an hour before dark and it must be every bit of a hundred and ten degrees out in the middle of the most God-forsaken country you have ever seen. We get back on the road again, and we are as lost as ever. She starts bitching right where she left off. She hates this story. She never understood any of it."

"Sir? If you don't mind my asking, what *is* the point?" Jackson asks.

"Bob," the President pauses. "Sometimes you need to top off your tank."

"I see."

"Bob, can I ask you a question?"

"Yes, sir."

"Do you believe in UFOs?"

*

"UFOs? Seriously?" Jackson's boss asks.

"Well, UFO singular, so yeah," says Jackson.

The head of the presidential security unit ponders that.

"I did not see that coming. You think he was serious? Is this some sort of put-up job or does the guy with his finger on the launch codes really think he was probed by the mothership?"

"I honestly don't know, chief," Jackson can't meet his boss's stare. "He was talking some goofy shit beforehand about a desert trip and a weird visit to a gas station, and then goes all Fox Mulder on me. I like the man. I really do. I think he genuinely cares about this country and is doing a great job. But this is way above my pay grade."

"This is above everyone's pay grade," the security chief says. "Let's say you forget he's the President for a minute. What would you do if this was a bowling buddy who started talking this way?"

"You know I don't bowl, right? I don't know. I guess I would be there for him and hope it's either a phase he is going through or a gag."

"What are you going to do if it's not?"

"I have no idea. If he really is cuckoo for Cocoa Puffs, I guess I try to keep his fingers off the launch codes," Jackson tells his boss. "I guess it goes without saying we never had this conversation."

"Oh, you can bet my pension check on it, sonny-boy. When I look into the future, I see a twenty-two foot fishing boat in my retirement which will never happen if anyone even suspects we talked like this."

"What would you do, chief?"

"I would talk to your friend and make sure it's a gag, avoid Richard Monteath like the devil himself," the head of the security detail says, "and hide the launch codes."

*

L MINUS SEVEN DAYS

"Osprey's on the move in the Nest enroute to press room. ETA two mikes."

"Roger, Bird Watcher Two. Copy two mikes," Jackson earpiece replies. His protection team follows immediately behind the Commander in Chief.

Richard Monteath intercepts them in the hall and matches the President's stride.

"Mr. President? Is there something I can help you with?" Monteath seems desperate.

"No, Dick, I'm 'bout to have a little chat with the gaggle," the President tells him.

"Uh, what about, sir?" Monteath nervously glances back at Jackson, who strides impassively behind his protectee.

"This and that. A few things I think folks oughta know."

"Sir, I don't think that's a good idea," the Chief of Staff grabs the President by the elbow, pulling him to a stop. Every Secret Service agent steps forward and tenses. "I have been with you since before you were a senator. We grew up in the same holler. I was the one behind you, helping you all the way into office."

"Yes, Dick, that's certainly true. You were behind me every step of the way and are still behind me now," the President looks down at the hand holding his elbow. "You know how I know that? That's where my coattails are. Now you can watch this from the door of the press room, or you can watch it from outside the gate. I am going to talk to the press. Your remaining choice from here on, is where you stand."

Monteath steps into Jackson's path.

The protection team turns to Jackson.

"You know the routine. Stay with Osprey. Give me a minute and I will catch up," Jackson tells the next-in-command. He turns to Monteath. "Sir, I respect your position as Chief of Staff, however, you have fifty-four seconds before I arrest you for interfering with the duties of a federal officer."

"For the love of God, Jackson, you can see where this is going. You have to stop him. He's going to bring down this administration and everyone in it."

"Forty-four seconds."

"Jackson, I am begging you. If you truly are his friend, you will talk some sense into him. You cannot allow him to make a mockery of the Presidency."

"I'm going now, Mr. Monteath."

"You were going to give me a minute," Monteath whines.

"The President walks faster than one would think for not being on both rails. Maybe it's the lack of weight on his coattails."

*

Jackson enters the press room from the back near the director's suite. Since the White House Press Secretary isn't expecting the President to show up and the news day looks relatively light, the technical suite remains unoccupied. Jackson has it to himself. He makes eye contact with the lead agent nearest the door and nods.

Press Secretary Neamans spots the Secret Service detail by the door and it throws her off a beat during one of her answers. As an aide steps toward her with a note, the President bursts through the door in a wave of Secret Service and strides toward the podium. Everyone clamors to their feet.

"The President of the United—" begins Neamans. She steps back to let her boss assume the podium. "States."

"Ladies and gentlemen of the press, good morning. Please sit down," the President begins. "Can we get you something to drink? Water? Coffee?"

The press looks around in confusion. Press Secretary Neamans' head swivels in a panic.

The pause turns the air painful with confusion.

The representative from the Times speaks up, "Uh, no sir." Then, almost as an afterthought, "Thank you."

"Smart people. The coffee here sucks. Now, where was I?"

Jackson casts about the director's studio in a panic. What to do? There's a fire alarm, on the other hand, it's a criminal offense to start a false alarm. Start one in the White House and you can kiss your Secret Service career goodbye.

"Anyway, did I ever tell you about the time the First Lady and I got lost in the desert? She hates this story. This was before she was the First Lady—" the President begins.

With his jacket sleeve covering his hand, Jackson slams the master breaker off in the circuit box on the wall of the director's suite. The room lights and podium microphones go dark. The room erupts in confusion.

"Get Osprey out!" Jackson barks into his wrist mic.

As one, agents surround the President and hustle him out of the room, bodily shielding him.

Jackson slips out the back of the director's suite into the West Wing bullpen.

In the near darkness, Chief of Staff Monteath is nowhere to be found.

Press Secretary Neamans collapses into a chair behind her. She didn't know it was there.

*

"Chief, it's Jackson—"

The phone goes dead.

Jackson redials the extension of head of the Secret Service detail.

"Chief, it's—" Click.

"Dammit!" Jackson snarls into his wrist mic, "Keep Osprey in WarNest. I am 10-76 to Bird Watcher One."

It takes Jackson five minutes to race to the office space the Secret Service chief uses in the White House. After a quick knock, he enters without waiting for a response.

"Chief—"

"Special Agent Jackson. Stop. Seriously. Say nothing. Answer my questions and nothing else," the head of the detail instructs him. The normally convivial detail chief shocks Jackson with his formal tone. Using the phrase "Special Agent Jackson," the detail head is letting him know about a hidden recorder.

"But Chief—"

"NOTHING! If I hear one word other than a simple, direct answer to one of my questions, I will put you on report myself. So, I am ordering you to stop your babbling." *Myself? Who else is listening to this*, Jackson wonders.

"Yes, sir."

"Is Osprey in any *immediate* danger?"

Jackson considers. The key word is immediate. The chief used the word "immediate" specifically. "No, sir."

"Is Osprey in Nest Actual?"

"No, sir, I instructed the detail to escort him to the Situation Room."

"That's correct. I confirmed those instructions from comms. I merely needed you to verbally and *physically* verify it," the detail chief stares at Jackson's eyes. Not at the ceiling, office furniture, or anywhere a person may casually glance in a natural conversation. *Physically? There's a video camera in here.* "Let me summarize the situation. The power outage incident in the press room was not any type of immediate threat, at most, an, as yet, unexplained accident, in which your team immediately and safely escorted Osprey to safety to WarNest? A yes-or-no question, Special Agent Jackson."

Jackson made no mention of the press room, yet the chief did. *Something strange is going on here. The chief is leading him.*

"Yes, sir."

"Very good. Make sure you write up your official report accurately and as we have discussed here. Email it to me at end of shift. Get back out there and protect the office of the President. Dismissed."

"Email"? While we do file our reports electronically, the chief prefers us personally handing him printed reports. And "accurately"? Since when do we need to be prompted on that? The key words here are "official report" and "as we have discussed here." The chief is telling me my report is being read by someone else and it better read in a way it won't get us both shit-canned. Or worse.

The one piece I can't figure out is: the chief told me to "protect the office of the President." He knows damned well we don't protect the office, we protect the man. Why would he tell me to protect the office?

*

Jackson reaches the Situation Room. The Secret Service does not have key card access to the most secure room in the world. The protection team used the President's pass card to escort him in earlier. After presenting his credentials to the Marine outside, the guard cards the door open. Jackson holds the door open while still standing in the hall. He has no authorization to enter without a pending threat to the President.

"All clear," Jackson tells his detail through his wrist mic. "Let's escort Osprey back to Osprey Nest."

The agents escort a shaken president through the door.

From inside the Situation Room, "Special Agent Jackson? A word, please."

What now? "Head back to the Nest. I will join you shortly," he instructs his team. He sticks his head inside to see who summoned him. Without proper authorization, he shouldn't be in there.

The Secretary of Defense, the White House Chief of Staff, and the Joint Chiefs of Staff. Okay. Properly authorized, it is.

He steps into the room and assumes full attention.

"Relax, Special Agent," the White House Chief of Staff says. Jackson assumes parade rest position with both hands interlocked behind his back.

"The boy genuinely doesn't get the concept of *relaxed,* does he?" Monteath says from his chair near the head of the table.

The admiral looks at the COS with a little disdain. "Dick, for a former Marine, what you're seeing *is* relaxed. We've spent the last 190 years or so making sure of that."

"Cain't he at least sit down?" Monteath asks.

"In front of *these* men? Not without a direct order. At ease, son. Rest."

"He surely doesn't care for the whole *son* thing," Monteath whispers as he watches Jackson move his hands in front of him and never changing his stance.

"I think he'll take it from me," the admiral whispers back. "Special Agent, I understand you've had a conversation with Dick here."

"Yes, sir."

"Did he ask you to spy on the President, son?"

Face frozen, Jackson's, eyes flicker toward Monteath for a microsecond.

"No, sir."

"Good answer. Most likely a whopper, so what the hell," the admiral looks at his notes. "We've reviewed your record, pretty damned impressive. Exemplary record in Marine Expeditionary Unit. Top of your classes at Glynco and Special Agent Training. Accelerated field office and fast-tracked into a protective detail during the President's first campaign. Bumped to protective lead in a couple of years. Son, if you'd have stayed in uniform, I'd be worried about *my* job."

Since the admiral hadn't asked him a question, Jackson remains quiet.

The admiral looks over at Monteath and lowers his head.

"Here's the thing, Special Agent, the Chief of Staff asking you to spy on the President was a mistake," the admiral's eyes bore into Jackson. "In actuality, we need to do is inject this into him."

*

"Sir?"

"Take a breath, son," the Secretary of Defense tells Jackson. "Dave, show him the ampule."

The CIA director pulls a small box, the size of old-fashioned cigarette case, from his briefcase, opening it and sliding it across the wide table to the admiral. The admiral turns it toward Jackson and he sees three plastic ampules the size of one-ounce eyedrop containers.

"From what Dave tells me, these three ampules each have a near-invisible needle on the end. You press one of them against him and squeeze. You don't even have to prick exposed skin. To get rid of them, the ampules themselves dissolve altogether after about minute under a hot water tap. Don't hold them very long in your bare hand. Your body temperature and sweat will start to dissolve them."

"Sir? You want me to poison the President?" Jackson asks. To his credit, his voice doesn't waiver when speaking.

"Poison? Oh hell no. These are mild sedatives," the admiral explains.

"They take a few minutes to be entirely effective, thoroughly dissolve in the bloodstream, and are impossible to detect after twenty minutes. About the same amount of time the subject will be unconscious," the CIA director says. "We had to trade off reaction time for untraceability. They act like propofol, though cleaner.

"The *subject*? You mean the President of the United States?" Jackson asks incredulously. This whole scene was becoming a James-Bondian psychotic episode. "I'm supposed to roofie Osprey?"

"Stand down, Agent. We are not asking you to walk up and dose the President," the admiral says. "We want you to try and reason with him. You are the sole person he trusts these days and we want you to make sure he is not going to jeopardize the government by saying something he shouldn't, like some ridiculous story about a drive in the desert. We're not talking about influencing the man on foreign policy or state secrets. We're talking about seeing if he will keep the woo-woo stories to himself. For a few more years."

"And if he insists on taking his story public?" Jackson asks the admiral.

"Well, then, I'm afraid we are going to have to protect this country's best interests no matter what."

"With all due respects, sirs, what you are talking about is a life sentence for me. It's all well and good for you to sit down here and plan your little coup, yet I'm the one who would be doing an indefinite stay at Casa Del Leavenworth."

"We have you covered." The admiral receives a document from an aide standing behind him. "We issued a signed document from everyone here stating you are acting under direct orders from us," he reads from the sheet, "*to incapacitate your protectee in the event he demonstrates any potential threat to the security of the United States, whether physical or intellectual.* I think it's safe to say we have had a lawyer or two take a look at this first."

Jackson takes the sheet and looks at it. After a nod from the admiral, the aide retrieves it.

"We've had a psychologist and psychiatrist listen to the desert story and both are willing to certify him unfit to serve, in which case the 25th Amendment comes into play and the Vice President takes office. You'll note he was elected to office, so the whole military coup threat you've been tossing around, goes out the window," Monteath gloats. "Even without the shrinks involved, we could use Section 4 of the 25th Amendment and force him out. Doing that, we have to present a declaration to the Senate and in the meantime, a conscious, out-of-control president could do a lot of damage."

"And as of now, we honestly do not have enough hard evidence of the President's mental incapacitation," chimed in the CIA director. "That's why we need you to keep a closer eye on him. We need you to be close to him, in case he starts to unravel."

"To be very clear, we want you to talk to the President, try to lean him away from talking like a lunatic to the public," the admiral says. "And if that doesn't work, knock his crazy ass out."

*

L MINUS THREE DAYS

"It won't kill you."

"Are you one thousand percent sure of that?" Jackson asks the lab tech.

"Well, *anything* in quantity will kill you. Hell, air in the bloodstream will kill you. Pump too much blood into a guy and he'll die as sure as a gunshot. The sample you gave me is a sedative. Administered in small doses and depending on the patient's blood gas partition coefficient, you might wake up a little groggy, however this is closer to the propofol end of the scale than sodium thiopental's."

Jackson had approached one of his buddies from the Secret Service's Criminal Investigator Training Program to analyze a drop of the fluid in the ampules. He could count on his friend's discretion.

"How much of a dose are you talking here?" the technician asks.

"Eh ... fifty milliliters. Like an eye drop container."

"Nah. Won't kill you. Knock you out for a bit and in fifteen, twenty minutes you'll be up and at 'em." His friend holds up the glass slide. "Where'd you get this stuff? I've never seen anything like this. I bet this shit dissolves in the bloodstream likes nobody's business. I know of faster acting stuff, but nothing that disappears like this. This is some covert OPs shit right here."

Both men make note of the fact of Jackson nonchalantly pocketing the slide from his friend's hand.

"Came across it in the field," Jackson says. "Tell me again this never happened."

"Dude, I don't even know who *you* are."

*

L MINUS ONE DAY

"Sir, do you have a minute?"

"Sure, Bob. Though don't tell those fourteen secretaries out there. Keeping me overbooked gives them reason to keep on living. What can I do you for?" the President leans back in his chair behind the Resolute Desk.

Jackson gingerly steps into the Oval Office from the veranda.

"You're not on duty now, have a seat."

"Yes, sir. You're sure I'm not disturbing you?"

"No. Hell. This peace treaty'll still be here tomorrow," the President jokes. "What's the matter, man? We've known each other going on six years now and never once have *you* asked to talk to me. Are you dying, Bob? Shit. Am *I* dying? We ain't lucky enough for the First Lady to be the one. Dick Monteath has already outlived cockroaches, so spit it out man."

Jackson notices the President's home state twang and vernacular has crept back into his voice in the last few weeks. You can take the Rhodes Scholar from out of the hills...

"Sir, I wanted to talk with you about our discussion a while back," Jackson begins. "You know, the desert story."

"Yeah, I am not likely to forget. What about it?"

"Well," Jackson hesitates. "were we seriously talking about UFOs, sir? Are we sure it wasn't weather balloons or experimental planes or something?"

The President grins and covers his smile with his hand.

"I guess I sounded crazier than a bag of hammers, huh? I bet the boys downstairs are pretty near shitting themselves. Lord knows the veep has already measured his backside to see if it fit in this chair."

"It did sound a bit peculiar, sir," Jackson says, starting to relax.

"It weren't no unidentified flying object."

"No?"

"I can identify what it was and where it's from and what they want. And tomorrow at about ten a.m., I'm addressing a press gaggle out on the White House Lawn to let everyone know. Screw the lights in the press room."

*

LANDING DAY, 0950 HOURS

"Bob! I need you in here right now!"

Jackson leaps into the Oval Office as he alerts his team and calls a replacement for his position outside on the veranda.

"Sir?" Jackson looks around at the Joint Chiefs of Staff and Richard Monteath gathered in the now-cramped executive office.

"Bob, your job is to protect me from any threats, right?" the President asks, never looking away from the Joint Chiefs.

"Yes, sir."

"Well, these pack of jackals have spent the last thirty minutes trying to convince me I'm crazier than a June bug and my best guess is they're ganging up to fit me for a jacket with no hand holes. You need to get over here, do your job and make sure I stay safe."

"Yes, sir." Jackson moves a step behind the President.

"Now boys, me and my escort here are gonna mosey on out to the rose garden and have a few words with the press. You fellas can start drafting those resignations you'll be handing me when we get back in here. First one on my desk gets a Nehi. I bet we can even dig up an orange one—

"Whatthehell?" the President slaps his neck.

"Sorry, sir," Jackson lowers the President to the carpet. "It really was for your own good."

"Bob? I trusted you boy," the President says quietly. "I know why they're here."

*

"OHMYGAWD! What happened to the President? Is he okay, do I need to call an ambulance?" One of Monteath's aids busts into the Oval Office door and sees the scene before him.

"It's all right, Jason. He's fine. What did you bust in here for?" Monteath asks.

"You have to see this!" The aide drags Monteath by the arm over to the glass doors of the Oval Office. "A crystalline spaceship touched down in the Rose Garden!"

As the Joint Chiefs crowd around the windows, the President still laying in Jackson's arms says, "I told you I know'd what they was here for. They're here to refuel and get something to eat. Sometimes, you just need to top off the tank."

***

The Dark Knightmare
Superhero, the fantasies of a comatose child, or something worse?

He crouches on one of the stone gargoyles that seem commonplace to the tallest buildings in the city. His city. Coiled as if about to strike, he appears nothing more than another silhouette against the night sky. He spies the signal lighting up the clouds, but the earpiece in his cowl is attached to a police scanner in his belt and he already knows of the problem. In a single motion, he leaps from the skyscraper, snapping his arms outward to convert his leathery cape to a paraglider as he falls. As he sails over the rooftops far below, his shadow and memory pass over the alley where it all began over a decade and a half ago.

*

"Dad, I know a shortcut that will get us to the car in no time," the young boy excitedly told his father, eager to impress. He and his parents were leaving a late-night showing of old Zorro films. They normally didn't allow him to be up so late, but it was his birthday wish. Unfortunately, his shortcut led the young family through a darkened alley.

The gunman stepped out of the shadows and aimed straight for his father's chest. The boy's eyes captured it all. Everything happened both instantaneously and incredibly slowly. The robber was so nervous, his gun shook as he held it. His father stepped in front of his son and wife. The gunman mistook that sudden move and fired.

"Thomas! No!" his mother screamed as the gunman fired at her in sheer panic. Her faux pearl necklace exploded with the impact of the round. Small white spheres scattered across the alleyway.

The thief, too scared to collect their valuables, ran. The boy sank to his knees over the still bodies of his parents and wept.

*

His soaring flight across the cityscape ends in a controlled roll into the midst of robbers exiting a jewelry store long after it has closed for the evening. With martial arts not often seen, he makes short work of the henchmen, but stops short when he sees their leader for the first time. A short, squat man in a tuxedo and top hat, carrying an umbrella, waddles out the front door of the shop. The leader begins to raise his umbrella. The man in the cowl snaps his left arm out to extend his cape and slashes across the face of the villain. Continuing the movement, he lashes out with a vicious spinning kick, catching the temporarily blinded, would-be robber directly on his ... monocle? Who wears a monocle these days?

As he binds the criminals to a nearby lamp post, its light long busted, he wonders, not for the first time, where they all come from. This city has always had more than its share of lowlifes and thugs, but in later years, it's as if the criminal population has become more ... extreme. The leaders recently all seem to have their own certain brand of either style or insanity. Last month, it was a lunatic dressed all in green who announced his impending crimes with nearly impossible riddles. Before that, it was a tall, voluptuous, beauty queen in a leather cat suit with razor sharp claws. He had to admit, she was pretty hot. Although literally, bag-of-cats crazy. Every crime she committed had a feline aspect to it. It wasn't hard to anticipate her next move. Now we have a formally dressed fat man, looking more like a gigantic Antarctic fowl than a human. After all that, he feels like the caped crusader of Crazy Town.

A call to his ally, Commissioner Jim, explains to the arriving officers why the perpetrators are bound securely next to the stolen goods outside the jewelry store. The rope he uses to bind them is a common nylon cord that cannot be traced back to his alter-ego. A device from the back of his belt allows him to scan their fingerprints, photograph them, and sample their DNA. He presses a hidden stud on his utility belt to remotely call for his car to retrieve him. The dark, bulletproof vehicle autonomously drives itself through the darkened streets to arrive at his location. His mansion is beyond the city limits and his ability to travel building by building. It's time he called it a night. After all, a growing boy needs his sleep. Even in Crazy Town.

*

"Sir, how was this evening's foray into the city?" his butler asks as he approaches his master sitting at an immense computer console. "Any minor wounds that need attending to?"

"Not tonight. I'm just updating the computer with the data of tonight's activities."

"Would you like some warm cocoa to help you catch a few hours' sleep in what remains of the night?" his faithful servant asks.

"That would be awesome, Alfred. Maybe some of those little marshmallows too." He strides toward the elevator, dropping articles of his costume on the floor of the cave, knowing Alfred will pick them up as he always does without a word of complaint.

*

The strenuous night's activities, and even Alfred's hot chocolate, do not help him get a good night's sleep. The dreams, nightmares really, begin just after his head hit the pillow.

*

"I'm sorry to have to tell you this, Tom, but the last several checks

23

have bounced," the man with the white coat, glasses, and mustache said. He was clearly pained by having to deliver the news, but could see no way to put it off any longer. The tension between the two men was almost palpable.

"I know, but you understand how hard it has been for me to maintain a practice…since this," indicating the stump below the shoulder of his right arm.

"Tom, that was over a decade and a half ago. You should have moved on by now," the mustached man said sadly. "Have you tried looking for any other kind of employment? There's more out there than just being a doctor."

"Nobody wants to hire a one-armed medic at my age," the man named Tom said quietly. "And minimum wage jobs don't pay enough to afford … this."

"You were never what one would call 'wealthy' and those med school loans were crushing, but surely you two have built up a little something since then?"

"No. Every extra penny we had, came straight here. Plus some we didn't have. Do you know how hard it was to ask her father for money? He didn't have a nickel to spare and still he gave what he could, and we have yet to pay him back."

"I realize it's been hard, but as much as I hate to do it, the hospital administrators are forcing me." His mustache quivered with his trembling lip. "We have to look at the more affordable state institution."

"Not—"

"I'm afraid so."

"But that's where they put the criminally insane," Tom pleaded with his friend.

"Right now, that's all you can afford."

*

He bolted straight up in bed, soaked with sweat, heart racing. What was *that* all about? It was difficult for him to comprehend the underlying issue as a lack of money. He had never been without, so poverty was as alien to him as something you might watch on TV. Why did those men look so familiar? Especially the one-armed man named Tom. He looked so old, haggard, and worn down. Maybe it was someone he knew when he was younger.

He buzzed for Alfred to gather his sour-smelling, sweat-soaked, satin sheets as he headed for the mansion's gym. He needed to work that crazy nightmare out of his system. Surely it has nothing to do with real life. It was just a nightmare. It's time to start his day.

*

"Sir?" Alfred calls on the household intercom. "The limo has delivered your dates for this evening's festivities. Will you be requiring the Lamborghini or the Ferrari?"

After a moment's thought, he presses the button on the intercom.

"Let's go with the Bentley. Not enough room in the Lambo or Ferrari for three after all."

"Very good, sir."

"I won't be out late, Alfred, but a billionaire playboy's work is never done. I have to attend certain events just to keep up appearances. It's a dirty job, but someone has to do it. Besides, I have other duties later tonight." There are times, with the exception of the death of his parents, that his life seems like a fantasy come true.

"As you say, sir." The family butler has perfected subservience to an art form. It would be difficult to imagine him as anything but a gentleman's gentleman, even if that is a bit demeaning.

It was a very different vehicle that races toward the city later that night. One with a jet's flame blasting from a center turbo in its tail and with black fins on its rear fenders. It is one of many black vehicles with a similar motif and special modifications. The car is so advanced it nearly drives itself, and sometimes does. The owner stares intently at the winding road leading into the heart of his city. Another night, another bad guy.

*

In a much different reality …

"I don't care if they's been tenants for twenty years, if they can't pay the rent, then out they go."

The gruff landlord stomps his way up to the fifth floor apartment. He had let them slide a couple times over the years, more out of the reality that the apartment house is a tenement that is one health inspection away from a wrecking ball. Then there is the fact that they had been renting that shitty little fifth floor studio with no elevator for nearly two decades and he couldn't find a soul in this vermin-infested part of town who would go near a walkup like that. Even at his generous rental price.

Growing up in the streets of nearby New Joisey taught him how to solve most problems with his fists. His daunting size, grizzled appearance, and half-chewed cigar completed the picture of a violence-prone misanthrope. And that was just in middle school. Had he completed his education, he would have likely been voted Biggest Bully. His demeanor and presence allow him to pressure almost anyone he meets. Especially his tenants.

"Enough is enough. They's is three months late on the rent and they's has to go. I don't care if he is a crip wit' a sad story and a brat in a coma. Nobody makes a monkey outta me. They's'll be outta here by this time next week or my name ain't Big Al Pennywoith."

*

They say the world is what you make it. But tonight, the city is different. On a rooftop perch, he checks the sensors in his cowl and the equipment in his belt and can find nothing to indicate a change. But he can smell it. Once his city smelled of antiseptic and flowers and now it reeks of urine, fear, and desperation. Maybe it's Crane again. He always did experiment with pheromones and chemicals. He makes a mental note to have Alfred check the asylum to see if Crane escaped. *That place is a revolving door. No matter how many I put in there, some always get out.* When he ponders it, even the manor and the Cave have that same smell now. He needs to analyze it for a potential threat. *Why would it be so pervasive? What has changed to make everything feel so ... corrupt?*

The circular light hits the clouds. The signal. His signal. He leaps from the roof towards police headquarters, thoughts of odorous changes and hidden corruption nearly forgotten.

*

It's the third major crime this month. This time, there are reports of a gigantic crocodile man. The crocodile man supposedly climbed out of a manhole, killed two city power workers, and vanished back down into the sewers. More than likely, someone's flushed pet surprised the utility repairmen, they accidentally electrocuted each other, and the now-dead flushee fell back into the manhole.

Despite the more likely scenario, Commissioner Jim's patrolmen are taking it very seriously: taping off the area, calling in crime scene techs, and questioning bystanders. He sticks to the shadows as he makes his way down the street to a different manhole cover.

Something is causing this jump in activity. You don't have to be the world's greatest detective to get the feeling it is concealing some other behind-the-scenes tension. It's like something you can't quite see out of the corner of your eye or can't remember when waking from a dream. You can almost hear the muffled screams of pain and fear in the city. Once he resolves this crocodile man problem, he needs to look into this other worldly vibe he is picking up on. Unless some other crazily dressed villain pops up and he has to deal with that. Someone more cynical might think the underworld was conspiring to purposely keep him from focusing on this new mystery. If there was someone more cynical than him in this world.

*

He falls unconscious on the enormous bed without even removing his costume. His cape and cowl lay on the floor for Alfred to pick up, but he just doesn't have the energy to take the rest of his gear off. The criminal activity in the city has tripled since his encounter with the problem in the sewers. It is so crazy out there, he is considering patrolling in the daylight, something he had never done. Part of his mystique and ability to inspire fear into criminals is being able to hide in the shadows and strike in the dark. But the bad guys figured that out and are operating in broad daylight now. He barely has time to eat or sleep, let alone investigate his hidden conspiracy theory.

To make matters worse, he has nearly gotten so used to the unpleasant change in smell in his world that he rarely notices it anymore. He wonders if it was all in his head.

Much like the nightmares he is having every night.

"Can't you do something?" the woman wailed.

"I don't know what else we can do," the man in the white coat, glasses, and mustache said.

She, too, looked very familiar, but he wasn't quite able to place her. Her hair was gray and whisper thin where you could tell it was once lush and full. She looked so drawn and wasted away, like an oncology patient after years of battling both chemo and cancer. The dark circles under her eyes betray a life of hardship. If he could only remember who she was ...

"There must be something," the one-armed man called Tom said. "You can tell this place is evil. Hell, I'm wide awake and even I am scared to walk through the halls. The screaming, the howls, even the smell of this place."

He awakens in mid-afternoon, his costume soaked on the inside, his nerves raw from the high-octane emotions of his nightmare. "I don't want to self-medicate. I sure as hell can't go to a shrink," he looks around the massive bedroom, "and now I'm talking to myself. Perfect. Well, *we* might as well go to work. We're sure not getting any rest."

*

The lack of even fitful sleep, underlying tension, and increasing criminal activity had stretched his nerves to the point of snapping. Add to all of that and he could once again hear the muted howls and screams as well as smell the stench of his city, like it was rotting beneath him. He was overdue to make a mistake. It will prove fatal. Just not for him.

A madman, once a city official, with half his face burned beyond recognition, had discovered his secret identity. He wasn't sure how the madman found out, but when he came back to his manor, after a night's patrol, he found the crazed villain sitting in his father's favorite Queen Ann chair in the library, with Alfred tied and kneeling at his feet.

The madman would not engage when he tried bantering, desperately trying to buy time until he could find a way to free his loyal servant. With sudden inspiration and without warning, he pulls his own cowl back to reveal his face and while the madman is in momentary shock, he whips an explosive boomerang at him. Whether it was from his jangled nerves, the increased howling, or his lack of sleep, he misses. And hits Alfred. The explosion decapitates the family retainer in an explosion of red mist. He doesn't remember the insane villain fleeing the scene or the next few minutes, he only remembers kneeling beside the still body and weeping.

*

"You've got to get him out of here," his father said. "This asylum is no place for my son."

"I agree with you, Tom, but without any money, we can't move him to any other facilities."

"Dr. Gordon, do you still *not have any idea why he is like this?" his mother asked.*

"The best we can figure is that seeing the two of you gunned down in that alley, an alley that he chose to lead you down, threw him into some sort of near-coma," Dr. James Gordon said gravely. "He may not even know you're alive. Given the state we found him in, he likely doesn't know that the shots left the two of you barely breathing, and you, Tom, the loss of your arm. The guilt and trauma of causing your 'deaths' have kept him in this state for more than fifteen years. My only hope is that he is dreaming of a world better than this. It would be the dreams of a ten-year-old mind that hasn't had a chance to mature, but hopefully, they are

pleasant dreams."

"But—but—"

"Thomas, I am going to be very honest with you. I feel like you and your family are more than just a patient's family. More than friends. We are guessing that the reason his skin is so pale is the lack of sunlight he has experienced in the last decade and a half. But over the years of treating him, we simply don't know why he smiles so widely or why his hair turned green. We just don't know."

*

He lifts his gaze from the bloody remains of his faithful servant and one dark thought crosses his mind:

"Who is going to clean up this mess?"

***

A Wheelbarrow Full of Honey
Will a redneck scientist thwart an alien invasion?

As alien invasions go, this was pretty spectacular. Even by CNN's standards. A while back, three enormous crystalline vessels with tubular projections, without so much as a "we've-come-to-eat-your-population," de-cloaked adjacent to a few of the largest buildings and skyscrapers in the world and systematically sliced and diced them from top to bottom. The invaders then used some sort tractor beam in the tube to consume the people inside as well as the rubble itself. Within an hour, three of the world's largest buildings and everyone in them, had ceased to exist. No debris. Just gone. Governments scrambled to deploy fighter jets and attack helicopters to every site, but by the time they arrived, the invaders had slid back into invisibility like an arm disappearing into a sleeve.

It was starting to make some of the science fiction I write look tame by comparison.

A single ship appeared again five days later to begin the same process at the CentralWorld Tower in Bangkok. This time, the U.S. aircraft carrier *Jefferson* was nearby and deployed airborne counteroffensives. Sadly, any missile, aircraft, or rocket approaching the ship was effortlessly vaporized long before it could even close on the alien intruder.

Eleven days later, three more alien ships returned and ingested the Aalsmeer Flower Auction in the Netherlands, the Beijing Capital International Airport, and The Venetian Hotel in Macau (and coincidentally, the thousands of people contained therein). The general population didn't seem to grasp that no city or building was safe. The news networks were having a field day.

Score: aliens, seven; humanity, zero. Well, technically, the aliens were up about forty-seven thousand, and we had yet to even see one "Martian," let alone kill one.

It was about then that a very serious-looking USAF Major Andrews (according to his name tag) showed up at my door in Huntsville, escorted by what looked like two German-mad-scientist-genetic-experiments-gone-bad squeezed into Marine tactical gear. I'm not *saying* these boys took steroids, but you could almost see the light bending around the gravity field their muscles were generating. I had secretly named them Laverne and Maxine. To myself.

"Travis Montgomery?" in a tone implying that he already knew the answer and that my one of my customary smartass answers would be frowned upon.

"Uh, yep." Who says I wasted my folks' money on all those doctorates?

"I need you to come with us now. Sir."

"Am I in trouble? What's this about?"

"Sir, I am not at liberty to say. We have been tasked with retrieving you. Immediately."

Andrews' uniform had creases you could shave with. I, on the other hand, was wearing the same jeans for three days now. When I subconsciously compared my 180 pounds of blond, less-than-athletic nerdiness to Major Andrews' fit and snappy appearance ... well, at least I was still smarter. And I'm still hanging on to that thought.

"Sir, please come with us now." You gotta give him credit for sticking to his script.

I reached behind the door to grab something and Laverne and Maxine pushed through, effectively surrounding me in a wall of muscle.

Handing the closest Marine my overnight duffle, "Easy boys. I've been waiting for y'all for a few days."

"You have?" It was the major's turn to be off guard. "The decision to collect you was just handed down this morning. How could you ...?"

"Seriously? The world is attacked by extraterrestrial battleships. Everything the military can do has failed. My IQ looks like an SAT score and I wrote the book on alien invasions. Literally. THE Actual Book. Even Laverne here could have seen y'all coming." I have a tendency to get snarky and obnoxious when I'm nervous. Armageddon and Marines showing up at my door push me right up to the real dickhead level. "Besides, who ya gonna call?"

Ignoring the Laverne comment, and with a face as straight as a yardstick, the major replied, "You'd be surprised. Sir."

*

Six hundred and ninety-six miles, one military flight, two helicopter rides, and what seemed like miles of corridors, I found out who you would call. The Andrew Sisters escorted me to a dimly lit conference room inside the Pentagon. A full bird colonel was addressing the room near a lit screen in front.

"Ah, I see our last ... 'consultant' has arrived. Ladies and gentlemen, some of you may know the distinguished Dr. Travis Montgomery from his books and work on TV. Since we've already completed the introductions, he can catch up later. Dr. Montgomery, if you will ...," the colonel said, gesturing toward an empty seat. It wasn't really a request. The entire group stared at me. Some dismissed me with a smirk, a very few made eye contact, and the worst looked away blankly as if I didn't exist in their universe; clearly not big fans of my work.

As the colonel brought the room up to speed on the three incursions, I looked around recognizing a few of the two dozen faces assembled. Darby Keaton, an English string theorist I had met at a TED conference a few years back, one of the few people I have ever met with true eidetic memory. (You do NOT want to play poker with this guy. Don't ask me how I know this.) Two seats down from him was Han Su Kang, a brilliant weapons designer from Korea. I had read everything this guy had ever written. Off the charts smart. Across the table was Tng Zte Guyen (or maybe it was Ng Zte Yn? Whatever! Something with a shitload of consonants). The kid's supposedly the Chinese Mozart of quantum physics. If you want a Unified Field Theory, this is the guy you would ask. Farther down the table, Irene McCrae, the reigning queen-mother of modern-day radio astronomy and the search for extraterrestrial life, looked up with a warm smile. She didn't invent SETI, but she's pretty high up on their speed dial. The walls themselves were lined with large screen teleconferencing video feeds from other scientists around the world. Holy crap! Is that Stephen Hawking?

Despite my drawl, smart-mouth, and "aw-shucks" routine, I can be a bright guy. Clearly, I was NOT the first guy they called to help them out. I was not even the SECOND guy on the list. In fact, it looks as if I may have been the LAST guy to get tapped. (Arrogance, thy name is Travis.) Normally, I am the smartest guy in the room, but with this group, I am barely beating out Laverne and Maxine. And truthfully, when I look up at Hawking's gaunt features on the big screen, I'm not sure I beat Maxine by all that much.

Clearly, they didn't call me here for my athletic build or rugged good looks. I have written a dozen or so books, some science fiction and some practical science. My second most popular, *When Aliens Attack*, the Discovery Channel made into a big budget, pseudo-documentary. Probably why the

Pentagon called me in. Thank God it wasn't because of my most popular book, *Zombie Contingency Planning*. That would have just been weird. I also have a "reality" show on National Geographic, *Good Ol' Geeks*. (Check your local listings for times.) On that, a few of my buddies, my grandpa, and I, build some practical applications of modern science over the course of a weekend. My personal favorites are a lunar module made out of old beer kegs and a death ray from a Blu-ray disc player. Then there's my day job as an actual rocket scientist in that little Huntsville space program we have down there. Add that to my three doctorates and I usually AM the smartest guy in the room. Until today. I wonder if I should go out and get coffee for these guys.

*

Colonel Attitude completed his summary and glared around the room.

"Okay, *Doctors*. Here's the situation. We have tried damned near everything we can think of to stop this shit and have, so far, come up empty. While we work with the military forces around the world throwing missiles at these things, you geniuses are going to sit in this room until you come up with a way to kill these alien bastards. Any questions? Good. Get to it." With that, he stormed from the conference room amidst the silence of a stunned Brain Trust.

*

Three days later, Colonel Attitude (turns out his real name is Dixon, but he'll always be Attitude to me) strode back into the conference room and while the room quieted down, folded his arms, and perfected his military-issue scowl.

"What have you got?"

Silence.

"C'mon people, someone speak up. What have you *geniuses* come up with to kill these things?" He said the word "geniuses" the way a Baptist minister spits out the word "whores."

Silence.

"You're telling me that this frigging Mensa club, with enough IQ points to be a damned zip code, has come up with *NOTHING*?!"

Even Hawking's respirator went quiet.

The colonel's voice suddenly got very low.

"What the hell *have* you been doing for the last three days?"

I was leaning against the wall and muttered under my breath, "Seating charts on the Titanic."

"What was that?! You! Pretty boy! Montgomery, right? What did you just say?"

It's amazing how the power of invisibility never manifests when you want it to.

"Uh. I was just saying that we have gotten a little bogged down in details."

"Be. Specific."

What the hell. It wasn't like it would be the end of the world if I offended some of the greatest minds on the planet would it? Oh. Yeah. Never mind.

"Well," I took a deep breath, mentally erasing myself from Stephen Hawking's Christmas card list, "most of the time was wasted arguing about who should be in charge. The Chinese representatives thought that since they had lost the most people, one of them should be in charge. Surprisingly, Dubai made a very substantial argument for themselves. Then there was the debate over whether we should keep monitoring outside events as we worked. Many thought that would be distracting. There was more discussion about how much communication should be maintained with their respective governmental leadership. As you came in, you interrupted an exhilarating debate about what should be on the lunch menu. Asian cuisine was in the lead, but a strong case was being made for vegetarian."

"Are. You. Kidding. Me?" the colonel's voice a bare rasp now.

"Hey. Don't look at me. I voted for a few of them six-foot submarines sandwiches." I took a sip from my Big Gulp. My straw actually squeaked. Oh, well. I didn't deserve to be in this room anyway. Send my ass back to Huntsville and let me build rockets.

You could see the colonel attempt to compose himself as the veins in his neck threatened to rupture all over the congregated think tank. Are faces supposed to be burgundy?

"Major," he spoke in clipped, controlled sentences, "send for two dozen box lunches from the closest cafeteria in the mall. Disconnect all TV, Internet, and media connections to this room. Coordinate resources to do the same to anyone conferencing in. If they refuse, pull the plug on their teleconference. Collect every cell phone and disconnect all land lines in here. Tell the guards outside to shoot anyone who steps out of this room, except for you and me. That includes restroom breaks. Oh—and Montgomery is in charge."

And the crowd goes wild. Not in a good way.

The assembled scientists began screaming at the colonel. I threw up in my mouth. A little.

"You cannot put this 'farmer' in charge!" the Chinese physicist, Guyen, screeched. "He is not even a real scientist. He is a poorly trained monkey on your reality TV, spewing out illiterate pseudoscience for hillbillies and writing ill-conceived science fiction for American trailer trash!"

"Hey! Hold on there! Who ya callin' poorly trained, panda boy? And that's *Doctor* Monkey to you!" I stepped toward the table to test my working theory that not every Chinese man could possibly be Jackie Chan.

"Actually, I *can* put him in charge, Dr. Yn," the Colonel interjected.

"GUYEN!"

"Whatever. Montgomery is it because he is very likely the only person in this room that cares less about your personal needs and egos than I do. He had the balls to speak up when the rest of you didn't. I figure, with his reputation, he has less to live up to than the rest of you egotistical Einsteins. And lastly, he is in charge, because I FUCKING SAY SO!"

Somewhere in there was a compliment, but strangely, I was not feeling the love.

The room went quiet as the colonel glared at each of the delegates. They, in turn, glowered at me. I looked around and couldn't find Laverne. On a positive note, however, I have now experienced the physical manifestation of the word "seething."

"In twenty-four hours, I will be back and I want a damned plan!" The hydraulic mechanism on the door prevented it from slamming. Almost.

*

It wasn't twenty-four hours. It was five. A much more somber Colonel Dixon trudged woodenly to the front of the room.

"Ladies and gentlemen, thirty-seven minutes ago the aliens struck again. This time they devoured everyone in the Sands Cotai Central in Macau, Berjaya Times Square in Kuala Lumpur, the Central Park Jakarta Complex, the Grand Indonesia in Jakarta, and The Palazzo in Las Vegas. Despite the buildings being only partially inhabited, thirty-three thousand lives were lost."

The room once again fell silent with a completely different tone. While we had been arguing about lunch, the aliens were getting ready to eat theirs.

It was several minutes before anyone could speak.

"Why would anyone be in those buildings? Don't they know there's an invasion going on?" asked Keaton, his English accent thick with strain.

"Because of the randomness of the strikes, people are trying to maintain a semblance of normalcy. The world is stilling turning. Maybe, they are choosing to pretend it can't happen to them. I don't know." the colonel said, genuinely confused.

"Prime numbers." It was Tng Zte Guyen.

"What?" The colonel seemed fogged in thought.

"The extraterrestrials think in prime numbers. The attacks only happen one prime number from the last. Five days. Eleven days. And now three days." Guyen's voice picked up a little enthusiasm. As did mine.

"He's right. Even the number of ships they use and the number of buildings they attack are primes. Three. One. Three. Five." I said. Damn. I hate giving that little Chinese prick any credit, but he *was* the first to see it.

Guyen was on a roll. "What's more, factoring the time zone differentials, even the amounts of time between strikes are prime numbers."

Colonel Attitude was back in the conversation. Barely. "Big deal. They are attacking the tallest buildings in the world on odd number days and hours. With no pattern. How does that help me kill them?"

"Prime. Not odd," Irene McCrae said quietly. "It won't tell you *how* to kill them, but it could possibly tell you *when*."

Something else was bothering me. "Not 'tallest.'"

"What?" The colonel barked at me as enthusiasm rippled through the room.

"You said 'tallest buildings.' They didn't attack the tallest buildings. They destroyed the *largest* buildings," I said a bit sheepishly. "Darby, could you list on the screen the list of buildings attacked?"

Without visible concentration, Darby typed the list of every building assimilated.

New Century	*China*	*1,760,000 m²*
Dubai	*Dubai*	*1,713,000 m²*
Abraj Al-	*Mecca*	*1,575,815 m²*
CentralWorld	*Bangkok*	*1,024,000 m²*
Aalsmeer	*Netherlands*	*990,000 m²*
Beijing	*Beijing*	*986,000 m²*
The Venetian	*Macau*	*980,000 m²*

Sands Cotai	Macau	890,000 m^2
Berjaya	Kuala	700,000 m^2
Central Park	Jakarta	655,000 m^2
The Palazzo	Las Vegas	645,581 m^2
Grand	Jakarta	640,000 m^2

While everyone else concentrated on the list, I was gripped by a nauseating sense of dread.

"You memorized the metric square footage of all those buildings?" asked the Indian delegate.

"Sure. Didn't everyone?" Darby seemed perplexed.

I turned to the colonel. Very quietly.

"Colonel Dixon, we need to evacuate. Right now, sir." I almost whispered it.

"Montgomery, what are you going on about? This isn't the Huntsville Elementary School. Do you know how many people work here?"

"Thirty-one thousand. Twenty-eight thousand military personnel and contractors, plus three thousand civilian support staff." Darby informed him.

I looked around for *my* support. Of course, it would be Guyen to get it first.

"Dr. Keaton, please provide us with the next building logically on that list," Guyen politely intoned.

After a brief search of his memory, Darby typed rapid fire:

The Pentagon   Virginia 610,000 m^2

"Oh, shit."

*

The alien tube slid from invisibility three days later, lasered (for lack of a better term) the Pentagon into sections and harvested them into the maw of its gigantic circular nose. The building was empty (taking nearly a full day to get everyone out), but the airspace above it was not. Everything from stealth bombers to cruise missiles were launched at the alien craft's force fields. My nephew described it as an "epic fail."

I convinced Colonel Attitude to move the Brain Trust to the Holiday Inn near my grandfather's farm in Alabama. Very likely the last place in the known universe an invading alien force eating large chunks of population would come looking. We took over the whole hotel. The conference room was our war room. Even the large teleconference screens made the move. The security detail had their own floor. The colonel loosened his restrictions and although we were allowed to roam a bit and have access to Internet and media, most of us stayed in the conference room, working the problem.

The Brain Trust focused, forgetting their petty squabbles. No real progress was made. We just didn't understand their technology. We couldn't shoot through their defenses. We couldn't see through their invisibility prior to attacks. All we had done so far was save thirty-one thousand lives. And lose a Pentagon.

In an act of pure rebellion and frustration, I snuck out. I called my lifelong friend Bub to come get me up in his Ford pickup and he drove us to my grandfather's. Bub raided the fridge while Pappaw and I walked his wooded fence line. In Bub's mind, the end of the world was just another excuse to mooch beer.

*

"Travis, you remember the last time we walked back through here?"

"Uh-huh." My attention was chewing the technical problems of cloaking a ship one-fourth the size of a skyscraper. My intellectual inadequacy to lead this group was eating at me. Plus, something was nagging me about *the last place in the known universe.*

Pappaw continued, "I tried to show ya how to steal honey from one of those hive boxes up on the hill with a straw without smoking the bees. Ya damned near got stung to death. Never seen a boy cry like that. Ya ever try that again?" For Pappaw, the height of humor is seeing a teenage boy cry.

41

"Nope. Never did." Maybe an electromagnetic field set just so could bend the light. But *I don't exist in their universe.*

"Son. Where's your head at?"

"I don't know, Pap. I guess it's this whole humanity-getting-eaten-by-aliens thing. I'm just a tad scattered." *Bub raiding the fridge. Invisibility never manifests when you want it to.*

"Nope. That ain't it."

"It's not? I could have sworn being in charge of saving the world was what was on my mind." I replied while thoughts of the invasion and the Brain Trust ricocheted in my head. *Gravity bending light. Shoot through their defenses.*

"Shee-it boy! Ya've been writing them alien invasion books since ya was growing hair on your winky. That ain't what's bothering ya. What is it?"

Could have lived without THAT visual. We walked through trampled cornstalks for a bit while I gave it some serious thought. The old man wouldn't take my usual bullshit as an answer. He knew me better than just about anyone and if he said aliens weren't my real problem, then by God, aliens weren't what was really bothering me. Pappaw always had a way of cutting to the chase.

"Ya know, Pap, that's the kicker. I've been writing these books, postulating about what to do if aliens attack, made a shitload of money off of it, and just found out: it was all bullshit. None of it happened the way I said it would. I'm used to having all the right answers. I'm just a good ol' boy who's going to be the reason a whole lot of people get eaten. I can't wrap my head around it."

Pappaw just smiled. Only grandpas can get away with a smile during an apocalypse.

"So, ya'll geniuses are the security guards and them alien fellers are the crooks, and ya'll are just mad because ya ran up on someone just bit sharper than ya'll are?"

"Uh, yeah." Again, doctorates not wasted here.

"Son, I ever tell the story 'bout the time I was working at The Plant as security and we had a feller making off every night with them empty burlap bags?" The Plant, as he referred to it, was the Marshall Space Flight Center on Redstone Arsenal in Huntsville, where Pappaw was part of the security force, ages ago.

"Yeah, Pap, you told me that story a million times ... wait! Did you say 'stealing honey'?"

"'Bout fifteen minutes ago. Y'alright? Ya look like one of them bees done crawled up your pooper."

"Holy shit! Pap, come with me! I think you're gonna save the world!"

"Well, Mammaw wanted me to mow the backyard, but I reckon I can do that later."

*

Back at the Brain Trust, I gathered the team together, including Dixon and Andrews. While Pappaw told his stories about honey and burlap bags to everyone, I made lists of action items and a shopping list of special "groceries." I handed the two lists to Han Su Kang.

"Can you do it?"

He looked at me. He looked at my grandfather. "Yes. With help."

"Add whatever you need to that second list. Price is no obstacle. And Han? We need them yesterday. Two days from now is a prime number."

I handed the lists over to the colonel and explained my plan. He listened. He looked down at the lists. "This is way over my pay grade, son. I need to get someone with stars to sign off on this. Maybe even the CIC."

"Colonel, if you run this through channels, there won't be time to make it happen before the next attack." I remembered now why I passed on military service. Not so good with the bureaucracy.

"Travis, I *have* to ask permission. What you want will land my ass in Leavenworth ..."

He looked Major Andrews dead in the eye. "... if I know about it." And handed the major my shopping list.

*

The alien device appeared just above Air Force Plant 4, near Fort Worth, Texas, two days later. AFP4 was formerly the eleventh largest building the world. As it stands right now, it's number one. For the next thirty minutes anyway. The colonel, Major Andrews, and I have it staked out in a specially modified Humvee about a quarter mile from the plant. The "ship" began dissecting the building, seemingly unaware that the thousands of workers inside of it had been evacuated for days. Even from where we sat, we could feel the roar of the hundreds of tons of concrete and steel rubble tumbling up into the vessel and the keening whine of the beam as it dragged it in. As it nearly completed devouring the building, I reached for the switch mounted to the jerry-rigged control panel in front of me.

"I'm sorry, Travis, but by law, I have to do that. It's government property and it can't be a civilian that flips the switch. Plus, I finally have my orders." The colonel leaned forward between the seats to reach the switch. "Oh. And the President asked me to thank your grandfather for the stories."

*

Two days earlier Pap *had* told the Brain Trust some interesting stories. Sometimes, even genius needs a kick in the shorts. Sometimes, brilliance doesn't need a degree.

"I'm not sure what the point of this story is. Fact of the matter is, Travis don't come out looking none too bright. But he said to tell ya, so here it is. A bunch a years ago, when Trav was just a teenager, I took him up on the north hill of my farm where we keep a bunch them white box beehives. Smart as he was, I figured he needed a bit of real-world education and mebbe a little humility. So, I tried to teach him how to steal some honey with a straw and mebbe get himself a little honeycomb outta one them boxes without having to smoke the bees down lower inta the hive. His Mammaw damned near whooped me silly for getting him so stung up. Anywho, I guess I figured it was the wrong lesson, cuz he ain't gone near one since."

Thankfully, he left out the part about me crying.

"But damned if he didn't bawl like a little redheaded girl from all them stings, though!"

Even Hawking smiled at that.

"Pap, tell them the other story." Not that I don't enjoy a bucket load of embarrassment as much as the next guy. Even Guyen was paying attention now. It was probably the part about me crying.

"Okay. So, it's the early sixties and I was working security at The Plant and we had some reports of a feller leaving out the side gate of a new construction area with a wheelbarrow full of empty burlap sacks. Well, the gate guard stops the feller and calls up to the office. They tell him they don't give a shit 'bout no empty cement sacks. The guard hangs up and sends him on his way. Next night, same thing. Same feller with a wheelbarrow full of empty sacks. Guard calls up. Gets the same duty officer, gets his ear chewed out for wasting his time about empty sacks, and lets the feller go."

"What has this to do with aliens?" Guyen asked impatiently.

"Not a damned thing." Pappaw answered back sternly, regarding the young Chinese genius as if he just fell off the short bus.

"So, night after night, this feller goes through the gate. One night, I come up to the gate just as the guard was getting ready to wave him through and asked what was going on. The guard tells me the story and I go over and handcuff the man with the wheelbarrow full of empty burlap sacks. The guard is flabbergasted and wants to know what I'm doing. As I walked the purpeetraitor away, I looked over my shoulder and said, 'Sonny, he weren't stealin' no sacks. He was stealin' wheelbarrows!'"

The Brain Trust looked at me in confusion. Oh, sure, quarks and quasars they get, but wheelbarrows? Irene was the only who started to smile. I needed them ALL to get this.

"Guys, do I really need to spell it out? Those aren't alien ships. They're straws. They are not de-cloaking from invisibility, they are inserting from another dimensional plane into ours, like penetrating a membrane ... TO STEAL HONEY. Invisibility would require a monstrous gravitational field to bend light. Other than their tractor beam, they don't seem to affect local gravity fields at all. When they disappear, they aren't turning invisible, they are retracting back into their own plane of existence. Like a straw pulling back through a soda cup lid."

Darby piped up. "That would explain why the volume of material they are taking is greater than the mass of the vehicle. It is not a vehicle, it is a conduit. Bloody brilliant!"

"It also explains the object never navigating in our airspace," Han said, almost to himself.

Guyen wasn't drinking the Kool-Aid. "So, they are using these conduits to suck out the people? Granted, these buildings contain the greatest concentration of animal protein and fat in the world, but surely entities smart enough penetrate a dimensional membrane are smart enough to capture humans without all this trouble."

Before I could respond, Major Andrews spoke up, shaking his head in disbelief.

"Guyen, you asshole. Sir. They aren't eating people. The aliens are eating concrete, steel, and glass. That's the wheelbarrows. The people are the sacks."

"And the bees." Is it bad that I really enjoyed the "asshole" part?

"So, how do we stop them?" Guyen couldn't stop being a jerk.

Hawking's electronically nasal, computer-generated voice buzzed. "We sting them."

"Exactly!" I continued. "We make them cry like little redheaded girls so much that they never touch another hive!"

*

Two days later: As the last of Air Force Plant 4 was sucked into the maw of the alien extractor, Colonel Dixon flipped the protective lid and pressed the button. The alien device withdrew into its own dimension a few moments later. If all went according to plan, ten minutes later a series of redundant timers activated by that switch would detonate a cascade of suitcase nuclear devices that Han Su had shielded from detection and secreted in the walls of the plant. There was no visible sign of detonations from where we sat. God, I hope I'm as smart as Pappaw thinks I am.

*

It's been ten years since the Pentagon was taken. Construction is almost completed on the new building. Pappaw spends most of his fishing trips telling his buddies how he saved the world. None of them believe him. Colonel Dixon was promoted to general. Guyen was given a medal by the Chinese government for *saying* he saved the world. We lost Dr. Hawking. Maxine and Laverne are living together in a small condo in San Diego.

I wrote another how-to book on alien invasions. I did a nice circuit of talk shows. Seems the government is not all that concerned that the aliens are monitoring The Tonight Show.

I still haven't gone back up to the north hill of Pap's farm. Maybe someday.

Yeah. No. Not gonna happen.

***

Upon A Star
Not your papa's Pinocchio

It was early spring of 2043 A.D. when I discovered time travel.
Well, in all reality, it discovered me (and by "discovered," I
mean "bitch-slapped"). I was studying to be an artist,
specializing in artistic wood sculpture, in a low-rent New York
City design school. In essence, I was working my ass off to
learn how to (what they call down South) *whittle*. My parents
allowed me to opt out of junior high to study art at the design
school on a work scholarship. (They then promptly moved to
Nebraska. Or Kansas. Somewhere far from New York. I'm not
quite sure where. My theory was: they would miss me the least
of my six siblings.) The school was a renovated brownstone
deep in the heart of the Bronx. I won't say "I was learning," as
the snotty art teacher only graced us with his presence long
enough each day to criticize our work as "plebeian" and then
stormed off for a mocha latte frappe with a double shot of
espresso. I was struggling late by myself one night on an
abstract sculpture in oak (and ready to trash the whole thing),
when a blue light shone through the window near my
workstation, blinding me till I passed out.

   I woke up on the floor, the morning sunlight from the

window piercing my eyes like sharpened wood chisels. (If you've ever had your eyes pierced by wood chisels, you know exactly what I'm talking about.) *Oh crap! I slept here all night and if it's morning, class will be starting any moment and here I am laying on the floor.*

I slowly rose to inspect both myself and the room. It was the same room, except it wasn't the studio classroom anymore. It was a ramshackle workroom, piled high in wood chips, broken furniture, and dust. My own clothes were ill-fitting, rough wool and coarse linen. And itchy. An old man walked into the workroom, glanced at me, and said, "Don't justa stand there, clean uppa this mess."

I would love to say this is a story about my adventures and time travel and how what I told you just happened (I honestly don't know). But, this is not *that* story. I am going to tell you a story about a wish coming true.

*

Once upon a time (that time being the early 1940s to be more precise), lived an old Italian immigrant named Geppetto. Geppetto was a woodcarver by trade. He came from a long line of woodcarvers—a skill little in demand these days (again, meaning the 1940s). One spring day, the wood carver walked into his little shop on the ground floor of his two-story brownstone, and saw his new apprentice named Jiminy. You know ... me.

"Don't justa stand there, clean uppa this mess."

Whatever had transported me a hundred years into the past (an interesting tidbit I learned later) also seemed to have made my presence a part of the timeline. I blinked. Then started cleaning. What can I say? I watched a lot of sci-fi streams and believed the best way for me to get back to my time was to go along to get along.

*

Being an apprentice was not all that different from my studies in art school. The distinction was: I was actually learning something. Old ("Master") Geppetto was a kindly, albeit stern teacher. I had to do all the grunt work of cleaning and fetching, so living in a completely immersive environment next to a master wood worker, I learned more than I ever could in art school. While the living conditions were harsh, the earthy smell of sawdust, the sense of accomplishment, the honestly appreciated hard work, and the trade craft I was learning, made it all worth it. As an apprentice, I worked for free (again, not at all different from art school). I received room and board (no pun intended though the food even tasted suspiciously of sawdust) along with gaining practical knowledge of the ancient Italian's craft. One major difference is: back in the 1940's, my personality would be considered "flamboyant," much the same way Liberace was considered "eccentric." Sexual orientation was not even a thing yet.

As for Master Geppetto, at night, he stewed in his room above his Bronx shop. He spent his evening hours staring longingly at the photo of him and his beloved Cleo. The loneliness stemmed from the loss of his dearest wife during childbirth, shortly after their arrival on Ellis Island. Both her and their stillborn son were the only family the old woodcarver had. The few neighbors he knew, had long since moved out of the shabby borough. A tear welled in his eye as he stared at the old black-and-white photo in a hand-carved frame.

Living in close proximity to the old man, I discovered his many layers. Loneliness was not Geppetto's only defining characteristic. He was also a decent whistler, self-educated, a bit near-sighted, a decent cook, prematurely bald, a good man, an artist when it came to wood working, and extremely poor. The latter, due to the aforementioned lack of interest in paying for custom woodcraft. He barely eked out a meager living and was months late on his mortgage. He still managed to find a few jobs here and there. There were days when the old man's loneliness was overwhelming. I tried to console him, though he never saw me as a replacement for his missing son and wife. I was little more than the hired help. Hired help he didn't pay, but still ...

*

Whether it was from loneliness, boredom, or a gum-sized packet of crazy, Geppetto decided to whittle himself a marionette companion, a "son" to talk to during the lonely hours of the rest of his life. He was between projects and had no wood scraps to use. He looked around his shabby brownstone to see what he could use. All of his furniture (that he hadn't yet sold off to pay the overdue mortgage) was wooden and hand-crafted, though the best wood in his home was the built-into-the-wall cedar wardrobe.

"Fah!" the old immigrant said, "I can't afford nice clothes anyway. Jiminy, be a good boy and pulla these boards down. I take down the door."

Several hours later, we had disassembled the wardrobe completely.

He meticulously carved and sculpted each cedar piece, sanding the finish to be as smooth as a baby's behind. For larger pieces, such as the head, he glued several pieces together to form the whole and then sanded and finished them by hand into a seamless whole. After multiple coats of lacquer, the grain of the wood shined like glass. The face was adorable, cute almost to the point of effeminate with a delightfully small nose. Each joint articulated far better than a human's. Everything from the fingers to the ears, perfectly symmetrical. Aside from the wrist joints, which he could never quite get firm enough as they flopped around, the marionette was his masterpiece.

Though I asked to help Geppetto in his woodworking of the puppet, he politely refused any assistance. I watched as the elder carver artistically and lovingly worked his creation. After he had completed his masterwork, I dressed the puppet in an old pair of shoes, short pants, shirt, and jacket too small for Geppetto.

In my own way, I grew to love the moppet as much as Geppetto. A very different kind of love, but love, nonetheless.

Looking out the window, Geppetto spied a shooting star.

"I wish you were alive to keepa me company," Geppetto told the figurine as he sat it in a chair in the corner of his workroom. "*Buona notte*, my little Pinocchio."

After Geppetto retired for the evening, I made my way through the workshop to clean up after him as I did every night. After picking up the master's tools and sweeping the floor of sawdust, I sat on a wooden stool and stared at the beloved mannequin. It was almost criminal something so beautiful could be just wood, glue, and screws. Like the woodcarver, I too wished it could be alive. Not only so something so lovely could live, but selfishly, so I could have a special friend. It was lonely being a hundred years from the future and not quite as "butch" as the other teens.

As I stared, an intense blue light shone through the window directly on the wooden puppet. I leaped back so quickly I knocked over the stool and bumped against the worktable, noisily rattling all the tools on it.

The puppet's eyes fluttered. Its fingers twitched.

"*You can become a real boy if you prove yourself to be 'brave, truthful, and unselfish,'*" a voice emanated from the beam, seemingly from everywhere and nowhere at once. The light shifted its rays toward me.

"*Jiminy, you were brought to this place to be his conscience and companion. If you lead him on a path straight and true (well,* true *anyway), he can become a real boy, and your heart will find its way home. Don't screw it up.*"

Pinocchio's eyes opened all the way.

*

The ruckus woke Geppetto. As he made his way down into the workshop, his glasses askew and his toupee on sideways, the blue light receded out the window. The old wood carver stepped into the doorway. As Geppetto adjusted his glasses and stared into the room, the marionette stood in the middle with no strings attached to hold him up.

"Pinocchio?" Old Geppetto asked. "How?"

Pinocchio leaped into his creator's arms. The old

craftsman hugged the puppet to his chest, his heart nearly bursting with joy. Without warning, the wooden boy snatched the toupee from Geppetto's head, squirmed from his arms, and bound to the middle of the room. After plopping the wig on his own head, he pranced around the room, laughing at the old man.

"*Mio figlio*, my boy, the old man said, his face burning red. "Why do you act this away?"

"Because-a chrome-dome," the wooden boy said his first words, mimicking Geppetto's broken English and accent, "it looksa better on me than it does on you."

And just like that, with a slight creaking noise, his button-like nose, grew an inch.

Geppetto, his embarrassment forgotten, stood astonished at the sight of the wooden boy's nose growing. Pinocchio's eyes crossed, trying to see the change. As for me, I might have peed a little. I mean a living, prancing puppet that talks? C'mon on! (Said the time-traveling, sexually confused, art student who listened to a talking blue beam of light.)

"Your nose. How did you make it grow?" Geppetto asked.

"I don't know," said the puppet, his teasing forgotten. "It just happened."

Geppetto pulled up a stool to the chair he had originally set the puppet onto, and the two of them faced each other all night. Geppetto asked questions, and Pinocchio answered "I don't know," which was the truth since he had only been alive for a short while. This was all too much for me. Time travel. Talking beams of light. Living, prancing marionettes. I did what any exhausted and freaked out apprentice from the future would do. I curled up under the workbench and slept. Maybe when I woke up this would just be a burrito-inspired dream. (Wouldn't that make for an abrupt end to the story?)

As it turned out, I woke in the morning just as the old man decided the wooden boy had no answers for him and he needed some sleep. As Master Geppetto wearily, and happily, climbed the stairs to his bed, Pinocchio looked at me.

"I can't be caught dead in these old rags. I deserve to look *marvelous*! Let's go shopping!"

Under that workbench was looking better all the time.

*

I tried to talk him out of it. I really did. You know how it is with these animated puppets. Once they set their mind to something ...

While unable to find any clothes the puppet liked, we did stumble across some custom-made jewelry in a nearby shop.

"Aren't these just *divine*?" Pinocchio asked, twisting his forearm to make the bracelets jangle on his wrist. The old storefront sold everything from antiques to furniture to hand-crafted personal items. The shopkeeper, an unscrupulous vendor by the ironic name of Honest John, must have thought I had brought a life-sized ventriloquist dummy into the store with me. From his wood grain and polished veneer, one could easily tell that Pinocchio (or "Pinny" as I had affectionately come to think of him) was not a real boy.

"Yes, they're scrumptious, Pinny, and ... we don't have any money to pay for them."

"But I want them." With that, he dashed out the door leaving me standing in the middle of the small shop, and a storeowner shocked that a ventriloquist dummy could run on its own.

After stammering a quick "I'll catch him" to the shopkeeper, I chased after Pinny.

As I turned the corner, I glimpsed him hanging onto the rear bumper of a huge Chrysler, turning and waving to me as it sped off.

*

I burst into Geppetto's shop, winded and gasping, just as the old man confronted the puppet about the bracelets.

"Where did you get them, Pinocchio?"

"From a store."

"You gotta no money. Did you steal them?" his creator

asked angrily.

"No, Papa." And almost before the words came out, his nose grew another inch, the wood screeching quietly. The puppet crossed his eyes; Geppetto only became angrier looking at the new development.

"Pinocchio, you tella me the truth. Did you steal those bracelets?"

"No, Papa, I swear," the wooden boy lied. Then pointing to me, he continued, "*He* took them and made me wear them out of the store. It's Jimmy's fault."

With that, his nose grew two more inches with the sound of nails being pulled from wood. His nose now stuck out like a dowel rod from his face.

"My name is *Jiminy*," I corrected.

"That's what I said," Pinocchio stated. *Creak*, his nose grew another inch.

The puppet looked at one of us, then the other, his long proboscis swinging first one way, then the opposite in a wide arc. I stood, astonished, both at his transformation and the lies he told. I expected in any minute for Geppetto to send me packing. It was Pinocchio's word against mine. The old man thought of Pinny as his replacement son and I was just some little street swisher who swept up around the place. Mentally, I was already packing my bags, then realized I didn't have any. Man. Time travel sucks. Geppetto just glared at the wooden boy, his hands on his hips.

The puppet cracked under the old man's stare. Not literally, you know ... emotionally.

"Okay, okay. I took the bracelets. Jimmy had nothing to do with it. In fact, he tried to talk me out of it," Pinocchio said, turning toward his creator, looking at the floor. And as quickly as it had grown, his nose shrunk three inches.

"It's *Jiminy*!" I corrected again.

Pinny turned to silently glare at me.

"I know whata you did. Honesta John recognized Jiminy and called me," Geppetto said to Pinocchio. "Not only does he want me to return the bracelets, I have to make him some free furniture to make up for it, or he will go to the *polizia*."

Pinny was thinking less about Geppetto's losses than he was about his own nose.

"Papa, I'm sorry," the puppet began. "Your toupee really does look better on you than it does on me."

His nose shrunk down to its original size.

*

Weeks rolled by with Geppetto spending all his time on the apparently appreciative Pinocchio. I smiled, watching the former lonely old man come back to life with the miraculously beautiful wooden boy. The blue light had kick-started three lives that night.

Several weeks later, Pinocchio woke me just as I had fallen asleep. Geppetto had long since retired for the evening.

"Jimmy, wake up. Since the old geezer has no money, we need to get some of our own," Pinny whispered.

"First of all, Master Geppetto is NOT an 'old geezer,' he's your papa," I replied. "Secondly, he gives us a roof and food, he teaches us how to turn wood into art—why do we need money? And once again, it's still 'Jiminy.'"

Despite my protests, it didn't take long for Pinny to drag me out and find some street musicians and start dancing. I trailed behind in the vain hope of keeping him out of trouble. With his articulated joints, he could perform moves no human could. Between songs, he grabbed my cap and threw it down so people could toss change into it.

A long, red and obsidian Rolls Royce pulled up to the curb to watch Pinny dance. The rear window rolled down, and a thin, feminine hand with several large rings beckoned for Pinocchio to come closer. I couldn't hear what was said, but before long, the door opened, and Pinny clambered into the back of the car.

"Pinny! No!" I begged.

"Go home, Jimmy," I heard Pinny's voice from inside the Rolls as it sped down the street. "I know what I'm doing."

"It's Jiminy," I mumbled to myself, the car long gone.

*

This next part of the story I learned from Pinocchio later.

"Come in, my pet," the lady told Pinocchio, as she tossed her black-and-white spotted fur coat onto the jet-black and alabaster speckled fur-covered divan. Tall and gaunt, wearing a slinky black dress, the most unusual facet of this strange woman was her hair. Cut at shoulder length, her hair was half ebony and half bleached, colorless.

The puppet looked around the penthouse, seeing only nearly monochromatic white decor with occasional splashes of dark polka dots. It would have been *divine*, except the air carried a pungent odor of wet dog and stale smoke.

As the tall, elegant woman swept toward a coffee table for a cigarette holder and lighter, she asked, "Would you care for a smoke?" Then, looking down at the lighter, "Ah. No, of course not, wood burns so easily. You *are* made of wood, aren't you?"

Pinocchio, still standing in the entryway, said, "Yes. Mrs. ...?"

"You may call me Madame De Ville. And you are? Never mind, it hardly matters. Are you wondering why I brought you here, my pet?"

"It's Pinocchio, ma'am," he stammered. "I figured you liked my dancing."

"Ha. How droll," the older woman leered with a shark's smile containing far too many teeth. "I have a penchant for three things: young boys, personal toys, and unique items. And you, my pet, are all three."

"Well, I—"

"Shhh. Follow me to the boudoir and let Madame show you the benefits of being a good pet."

*

A few weeks passed, and Madame De Ville lavished presents and clothes on the wooden boy, and while he enjoyed her gifts, he was obviously reticent in entertaining her more carnal expectations. He just wasn't built that way.

"Seeing as how you were not carved to accommodate all my intimate needs, let's see what you *can* do," said the lecherous woman as she pushed his face far beneath the covers and between her nearly emaciated gams.

Frowning from his evident inexperience and reluctant efforts, she gasped, "Do you truly love me, my pet?"

A muffled "yes" and a creaking noise came from beneath the black-and-white fur comforter.

And with that, Madame De Ville squirmed and cried out, "OH MY!"

*

Several weeks later, a fat and hideous man with a long, dark beard was meeting with Madame De Ville.

"Pinocchio! Come here my pet," De Ville demanded. "You will be going with this man."

"W–why?"

"You obviously don't enjoy my company nor my sensuality, and frankly, I have tired of your lack of enthusiasm, despite your ... let's say ... nasal talents. Mr. Mangiafuoco has need of a creature with your abilities. While you are still rather unique, I prefer my boys and toys to be more ... satisfying. Besides, your wood grain clashes with my decor."

"What about my clothes and gifts?" the puppet whined.

"Oh," Madame De Ville said, "I will be returning those for a full refund. After what Mr. Mangiafuoco paid me for you, this whole fiasco will be nothing more than a faded memory in no time."

"You sold me?" Pinocchio gasped. "You can't do that! I'm a boy!"

"No, my pet. You were always just a toy."

*

Master Geppetto and I wandered the streets of New York for weeks looking for Pinocchio. We split up to cover more ground. I took Midtown, just south of Central Park, and

Geppetto looked south toward the Lower East Side and Little Italy, thinking there would be less of a language and cultural barrier for him. Manhattan was a big place to search for someone who didn't wish to be found. On the other hand, how hard could it be to find a living, talking puppet? We decided to check in at Geppetto's shop every few days to see if the other had any success. The poor old man was distraught over the loss of his creation. He hadn't worked in weeks and weeks, and had barely eaten or slept, looking for the boy.

The gloomy brick and wood structures had yet to make way for the gleaming towers of my time. The cars were as big as tanks, belching nauseating exhaust fumes, and nearly everyone smoked. Every man wore a hat and every woman, a calf-length dress. Despite how long I had spent in this timeline, some things never ceased to amaze me.

As I turned a corner, an old moving truck passed me with an advertisement papered on the side. "M's 'The Puppets Take New York.' A Broadway musical like no other." A painted picture of Pinocchio stared back at me.

Even though I knew Master Geppetto was in the general direction of Broadway, glass-enclosed phone booths littering every street corner were decades away. Several more decades would pass before pay phones were replaced with the ubiquitous cell phones. With no way to contact him or even know where he was, I did the only thing I could do. I set off on foot toward Broadway.

*

It took me days to find the right theater. I was way past my check-in deadline with Geppetto, yet I was too close to finding Pinny to backtrack. Far from being The Great White Way, it was more like The Downtrodden Sad Path. The playhouse was technically on Broadway, tucked down a seedy alley in a decrepit building. I convinced the owner, a Mr. Mangiafuoco, to take me on as a stagehand by nearly working for free. The cheapskate immediately took me on and fired a teen he was paying only slightly more. It wasn't hard to find Pinocchio's room. It had a paper star tacked crookedly to the door.

"Pinny? Are you in there?"

The door swung wide, revealing Pinocchio and a sparse room not much larger than a storage room. This was not the Pinocchio I knew. His lustrous sheen had dulled. His beautiful wood grain had faded and become almost ashen. His once gorgeous eyes looked sunken with circles beneath them. If it is even possible for a stick boy to get thinner, he had. A shadow of his former self or not, my heart still raced at the sight of him.

"Jimmy!"

"It's—oh, never mind. What are you doing here? We have been looking all over for you," I told him. "I thought I lost you."

"I'm being fabulous," the puppet announced. "See the star on the door. I am the talk of Broadway. I'm the one everyone comes to see. Come in. See my personal dressing room."

We both could hardly fit into the tiny room which smelled of turpentine and bleach. His stick-like frame was nearly pressed up against me. In more ways than one, it was uncomfortably close.

"We need to go home. Your papa is worried sick."

"Why would I go back there? I'm making new friends here. I'm having fun. I'm the star of the show. What am I to that old man besides a hobby?"

"Where have you been all this time?" I asked.

He told me the story of Madame De Ville and his joining Mangiafuoco's Broadway show.

"You idiot, you didn't join. She sold you!"

"You say potato, and I say stilettoes. Regardless, I am not going back to his workshop in the Bronx," he exclaimed. "I'm never leaving. Here, I am somebody."

"Here, you are making an ass of yourself!"

Doing a passable imitation of a donkey's bray, he pushed me out of his so-called dressing room.

*

I watched from backstage as Mr. Mangiafuoco directed his puppeteers to animate their marionettes. Mangiafuoco pushed his troupe to perform two to three shows a night. The tightwad refused to hire professional singers and voice actors, so the puppeteers had to perform vocally as well as make their puppets dance and act. To Pinocchio's credit, he was a far superior dancer than the string-controlled marionettes, though his voice was nothing to jump up and down about. The audience politely applauded after his routines, squinting to locate the strings holding him up.

After each performance, Pinocchio would disappear for several hours with some of the half-dressed chorus boys from the other shows. I was both jealous and horrified. He usually returned, barely in time, to take to the stage to do his part, always smelling of smoke, alcohol, and chorus boy.

"Pinny, stop whatever you are doing," I begged him. "It is killing you."

"I feel fine," he said, as his nose grew an inch with an audible squeak.

"Well, to be honest, you look like you are rotting from the inside."

When Mangiafuoco asked about his whereabouts and what he was doing, Pinocchio would say "Nothing." And his nose would creakingly grow another inch.

Afraid to leave Pinny, I had finally spoken to Geppetto. He had returned to his shop several times to check in and I finally was able to catch him on the phone. (I may, or may not, have broken into Mangiafuoco's office to borrow the phone. Hey! It was a local call.) Before I could tell Pinny what I had learned, he disappeared with his friends again. Pinny finally stayed out so long he missed the second show entirely, staggering back in only to run into Mr. Mangiafuoco outside his office door.

"I'm done with you, Stick," the show owner bellowed. "You aren't worth the trouble of the few people coming to see you."

"Fine," yelled Pinocchio. "Just give me the money you owe me, and I'll go be a star somewhere else."

"Owe you? After I spend money on your costumes and don't charge you rent on your little room, you owe me! Besides, I didn't *hire* you. I *bought* you! And I can see now, I paid way too much."

Pinocchio glared at the large man, "You haven't paid ... yet."

I noticed his nose didn't grow as he said it.

*

I followed Pinny to his dressing closet.

"Pinny, I have to tell you something. It's about Geppetto," I started.

"What now? Did he get a splinter?" the puppet asked angrily, his confrontation with Mangiafuoco still burning.

"No. All the time he spent looking for you, he wasn't working. Without work, he couldn't afford to pay the mortgage he was already months behind on, and now they're taking his home and shop away from him. He was so far behind, yet so close to paying it off. That's been his home for decades. The bank is just using this as an excuse to keep his money and take the building."

Pinocchio sat silently for a few moments on the only stool in the room.

"Didn't he and his wife live there right after they moved from the old country?" the puppet asked. The wooden boy's face couldn't adequately convey his concern for the old man. A concern that he was shocked at admitting to himself.

"Yes, and where he created you from a cedar wardrobe. You know that was the nicest thing he owned, right?"

"No. I didn't know that. I've been such an *idiota*. I need to get back there. Now." After a few moments of contemplation, the wooden boy's face turned grim. "It's time to show Mangiafuoco this one time, cedar can be a hardwood."

*

"FIRE!"

Mangiafuoco burst out of his office, grabbing a nearby bucket of sand on his way to the back of the stage. In an old wooden building where wooden and cloth puppets are the money makers, a conflagration can be a disaster.

As Mangiafuoco rushed past, Pinocchio slipped into his office and grabbed the satchel containing the gate for the last month. Dashing out the front of the theater, he met me running from the back. Without a word, we started north for the Bronx. It seemed like the exertion was a struggle for Pinny who just weeks earlier was dancing wildly on the streets of Manhattan. Extracting a single bill from the bag, Pinny paid for our bus fare to give us a chance to catch our breath (well, my breath anyway, I don't think he actually needed to breathe) and to get us there faster.

We ran from the bus stop after crossing the Harlem River. I lugged the satchel as it was simply too heavy for Pinny and he wanted to run to Geppetto as fast as he could.

From the corner, we could see the wrecking ball pulling back to swing toward Geppetto's home. The old man stood staunchly in front of the building, clutching the hand-carved frame with the picture of him and Cleo. Pinocchio raced and shoved the old man out of the way just as the ball swung toward the building. The steel ball only grazed the wooden boy, but, given his weakened state, it was enough.

With a sob, Geppetto picked up and cradled the puppet in his arms and carried him toward me. He sat him against a building to make him comfortable.

"Papa, I am so sorry," the puppet whispered. "I have been a horrible son. All I ever wanted to be was a normal boy. I guess I just never knew what normal was. Jiminy, give me the bag. Papa, in here should be enough money to pay off your mortgage, so you never have to worry again. Please forgive me."

His nose shrunk to its original button shape. The puppet's eyes closed.

"Buona notte, my little Pinocchio." The woodcarver said as a tear rolled from his eye to land on the wooden boy's face.

Fate still had plans for the Geppetto family. Just as a blue light shone down from the sky, Master Geppetto clutched his left arm and fell back on his haunches. The loss of his second son was simply too great for the old man, and despite what the doctor said later, I genuinely believed he died of a broken heart.

The blue light bathed the wooden boy, intensifying as it shone.

"*You have finally proven yourself to be brave, truthful, and unselfish,*" the voice from the light said.

As I watched, the wood grain faded to a natural skin tone. His lips softened. His hair transformed into real strands. Pinocchio's eyes opened and he struggled to move. I helped him sit up.

He turned and saw his papa slumped next to him. It was his turn for a tear to roll down his cheek.

*

One Year Later

In my own weird way, I was headed back to the future, one day at a time. The sign above the storefront read "Geppetto's Son & Associates Custom Woodwork – Where good things come to life." (Hey! It was the 1940s, I beat them to the punch by a mile.) I spent the last year teaching Pinny everything I had learned from the master. Business was good. With most grown men going off to war, a new need arose for skilled woodworking. A lady from the government came by one day to investigate two young boys living without adult supervision and the (under-the-table) gift of an ornate end table made that problem go away. Pinny worked hard at learning and honoring his father's craft and legacy. The money from the theater more than paid for the damage done by the wrecking ball, plus a few extras. Turns out, we didn't even have to add any rooms. With the mortgage completely paid off, we split the profits evenly, and a few well-placed (one could almost say *prophetic*) investments kept us in the black. Life was good.

"Did you hear about Mangiafuoco?" I asked Pinny while we worked.

"No. What?"

"Seems after the puppet theater burned down," I said, "Mangiafuoco filed a highly exaggerated insurance claim, ran off with the money, and now an insurance dick is after him. Last I heard he was in Nebraska or Kansas or somewhere far from New York."

*

In the middle of a lesson about burnishing, Pinny looked at me. The boy could buff a good piece of wood like he was born to it.

"Jiminy, why do think I still feel so different from normal boys? Neither of us act like the other boys our age."

"First of all, what is 'normal'? Stop comparing yourself to others and just enjoy who you are," I told him. "Besides, given the circumstances of your creation, how *could* you be like all the other boys?"

"What do you mean?"

I looked at him and smiled, "After all, your papa made you 'out of the closet.'"

We laughed and hugged for several long minutes. Not nearly long enough in my mind. I knew in my heart it wasn't only Geppetto's wish the blue light granted back then.

(I guess it goes without saying, we lived happily ever after. Too bad. I said it anyway.)

***

More Powerful than a Locomotive

*Retired reporter from a metropolitan paper catches her
extraordinary husband flying off to save the world*

He would be lying if he said that he didn't mind giving up
being a celebrity. Just once in a very great while. And he tries
not to lie. Flying around the world, flexing his power, getting
his way, nothing could stop him. It often made him feel nearly
invulnerable. It's true that *everything* he had done in his past
wasn't totally in line with "Truth, Justice, and the American
Way," but all those moments were long behind him. She had
changed him completely. More than that. He wanted to be a
better man FOR her.

He once thought he was the smartest, most powerful,
person alive. Until he met her. He could explain how
molecules interacted, how universes were formed, but she
understood how people worked. She had a humanity about her
that he would never match. He loved her for years before
actually telling her. Holding that truth in was the hardest thing
he had ever done in a lifetime of unbelievable feats. There were
obstacles to their life together. One particularly large obstacle.
Eventually, it was her, not him, who overcame that problem
and their relationship blossomed.

The feelings he had for her were more powerful than anything he had ever known. At one time, he was considered high above almost everyone, and now all he wants is to be by her side.

He remembers the day Lo told him they were going to have a baby. Other than the day Jonathan was actually born and the day they got married, this would forever remain the happiest moment of his life. He immediately told her that he would give up his other life. Forever.

"You don't need to do that," she said.

"I do. My new mission in life is to protect our new family."

*

RETIRING

He, in his more public persona, held a press conference later that week, but gave the exclusive interview to his sweetheart. In his press announcement, he simply said he was retiring from the world at large and that he had new priorities. As far as everyone else was concerned, he would merely disappear. Harder than it may sound for someone as publicly recognizable as he was, but not impossible, given his earlier feats. One day he was everywhere, the next he pulled a Howard Hughes.

*

"Chief ..." she began.

"Don't call me 'Chief,'" her editor snapped. "Whatever you want to expense or wherever you want to go, the answer is No!"

"It's not that—" she started again.

"What is *he* doing here?" He turned toward her husband. "Are you here for moral support or to be the muscle?"

"No, sir. I think you should listen to what she has to say," he said timidly.

"Well? Out with it. What kind of fantastic nonsense do you want to cover this time?" the editor asked.

She looked at her husband. She turned her gaze downward.

"I'm quitting."

"WHAT! Very funny. You couldn't live without the thrill of chasing of some story. What do you think you could do? What kind of joke is this?"

"We're going to have a baby," she said quietly.

For the first time in ten years, the editor was speechless.

"I'm going to leave in about two months, before I really start to show. We want to focus on raising a family and maybe write a few books. Besides, you don't need me around here. You're constantly saying how I eat up your salary budget and we both know things in print journalism are getting tighter and tighter." She didn't go so far to say that print journalism was dead, but danced all around it. It helped that Perry had passed on a few years earlier. She didn't know if she could tell her former boss to his face. Perry would never have accepted that his best investigative reporter abandoning him.

She insisted that if her husband could give up his life and identity to raise a family, retiring from the life of a reporter was the least she could do.

Finally, the editor could speak.

"Great Caesar's Ghost!" he turned to her husband. "So, this was what that press conference was really about the other day! Is this about more money? I could—"

"No, Chief, it's not about money. You know very well that with his resources and abilities, we will never have to worry about money ever again. We're having a baby and investigating stories the way I always have is just too dangerous for an expectant mother. It's time for a new chapter. This is about focusing on what's important now."

The editor looked at each of them.

"Well, I wish you the best of luck," and squared his shoulders, "But, don't think I'm going to take it easy on you traitors for the next few months. And I mean both of you! Get out there and find some news! And you," pointing his unlit cigar at her husband, "go do whatever it is you do. It's obviously not working for a living. Whataya waiting for?"

"Yes, Chief," they said in unison.

*

As soon she told him she was pregnant, he flew to Switzerland and the Cayman Islands and established new, untraceable bank accounts for them, trust funds for the baby, and had their wills re-worked. From now on, he wanted to live under the radar. Way under the radar.

*

That anonymity wasn't always appreciated, especially by a certain Kansas City bank manager.

"Ms. Siegel, what is this?"

"It looks like a cashier's check, Mr. Schuster. Made out to the bank," the lead teller at the Kansas National Bank said. "Based on the memo, I would say it's to pay off a mortgage."

"But there's no sender's name and it's drawn from a bank in Europe," the bank manager stammered. "This is all highly irregular. What am I supposed to do with this?"

"Looks like to me, all we *can* do is pay off the mortgage and send this lady the deed."

*

"New bank accounts, huh? What about your rule of always telling the truth?" his wife asked him when he returned.

"I didn't lie. I gave the Swiss banker my birth name, and I am fairly certain he recognized me. I may have done some business there in the past. None of that money was obtained illegally. And for the record, I didn't say 'always.' There are times when I need to protect our identities and I may have to genuflect a bit."

"So you just paid off Ma Kent's mortgage just like that?"

"And hired a neighbor to help with the chores. And created a savings account for her. I only did it because I know how you feel about her. I guess I should have talked it over with you first."

"Damn skippy you should have! Why didn't you insist she come live with us? I love her to death and who has more experience taking care of a special child more than she does?"

"Honey, I *did* try to get her to move in with us, but she won't give up the farm and the community she's lived in for decades. When she wouldn't move, I did the next best thing I could think of. She did say she would come for extended visits to help out. Sorry again."

"Don't be obtuse, Boy Scout. Technically, that's your money, but even so, you did exactly the right thing. Like you always do. Is it hard being so perfect?"

"It *is* a curse. And you know I hate it when you all me that."

"Why do you think I do it?"

*

Thanks to her Pulitzer and her well-(and sometimes self-)publicized exploits with his former identity and his adversaries, every major publishing firm in the country was in a bidding war to contract her story. Her agent procured a sizable advance which further concealed their actual net worth. They honestly declared all her income, including the advance for her book, on their taxes. Their finances would not bear up under intense scrutiny, but who was going to look closely at the tax returns of Mr. and Mrs. Joe Average? She was careful to separate her written exploits from their current life. She refused to do book tours, but it was hardly necessary to make the book a best seller, with both of their past adventures.

*

SOLITUDE

The couple bought a home in the Florida Keys to be as far away as possible from any temptation to investigate unusual stories and to avoid any tempting criminal activity. They purchased the home under their newly assumed identities.

They paid cash for the house, which raised an eyebrow with the realtor, but avoided a pesky credit check. They needed to buy a home and not rent so they could make some extensive renovations to it. She moved in upon leaving the paper and he commuted in his own unique manner. She worked on her book, in a secluded, rented office in nearby Islamorada, while he renovated the house as quickly as he could. He quietly called in few of his past associates to help with the more laborious and technical aspects. They were more than eager to assist the happy couple. Someone had escaped "The Life" and was going to be part of a normal family. Well, mostly normal.

He insisted that every room have red solar radiation emitters in the ceilings, just in case. He powered those through solar panels on the roof. A nice touch of irony, he thought. Solar-powered protection.

Thanks to his familiarity with high technology, the house was kitted as the smartest smart-home ever built. Besides voice commands, the home's AI often anticipated their needs and was programmed additionally for the baby's safety.

While she was busy writing offsite, he installed some discreet and passive defensive measures in the house such as Kevlar-tungsten-lead alloy reinforcement behind the sheet rock. Bullet and radiation resistant glass in the windows and titanium cores to the doors. Radar, sonar, and slightly more exotic sensor arrays monitored the skies, sea, and land around their new home, practically a fortress. Less passive were the futuristic weapons systems hidden in the landscaping. He didn't *hide* these alterations from her, but also didn't tell her about them. He didn't want her to worry about his past coming back to haunt them. She had enough on her plate with a baby on the way and a book to write. She would have thought all these precautions ridiculous, but there was someone in both their pasts who all these preparations may not be sufficient. Someone who may hold a grudge. Besides, who doesn't have robotic, Krypton-powered laser cannons retracted into the front lawn?

Along with the more discreet features of the house, they installed a panic room (which she insisted they call a "secure-room," because *she* doesn't panic). The room hosted a multitude of security monitors to scan both the interior and exterior of the home, an independent, uninterruptible power source, and was large enough, and stocked so well that they could stay there a very long time if need be.

*

LOOKS AIN'T EVERYTHING

Given her status as an up-and-coming best-selling author and their pasts, they decided to alter their appearance to further obfuscate any connection to their previous lives. Before any changes, she had plenty of publicity photos taken for her book jackets. She wouldn't look that way for a long time. She published the book under her original name, but lived in her new identity. Kind of a nom de plume in reverse.

He hired specialists to help with their transformations. Thanks to his past life, he was very familiar with people who specialized in both secret identities and discretion. She had her hair cut extremely short and colored sunny blonde. Coloring his hair was a bit more problematic, so he opted to go with a strawberry-blond wig that was so realistic, she had a hard time telling it wasn't his actual hair. He also grew a Van Dyke beard to further change his appearance. She thought it ironically made him look slightly villainous, but she couldn't deny it changed the shape of his jawline and hid the dimple in his chin. She jokingly suggested he wear glasses and a withering look from him ended that suggestion. A fake earring stud and colored contacts completed the transformation. She even let him smoke an occasional cigar, which he found surprisingly relaxing, as long as it wasn't in the house or near her. Add a colorful Hawaiian shirt and it all added up to a man not even his own mother would recognize. He would still have to slump to hide his physique, but he was used to creating that illusion, so people would constantly underestimate him. Eventually the wig would get phased out, but not for a while. The public's memory of him needed to fade a bit. Okay, it may take more than a bit.

*

DAY OFF

The couple took a rare day off. Funny how busy they were for two, supposedly, retired people. Her first book was off to the publishers for a final review, and she was well on her way to outlining the second. Her baby bump was more than showing, but they decided that they wanted to spend the day off at the beach. He ignored the impulse to joke about "being as big as a whale." It probably saved his life.

"You know, honey, we could just buy up all the property around us so we could have it all to ourselves," he suggested, eyeing her for her reaction. "In fact, we could just buy the whole Key."

She reacted poorly to that suggestion. The beach remained public to property owners and their guests.

He stretched on his beach chair. The sun's rays seemed to energize him and revitalize his strength. In his past life, he never really took the time to just *sit* in the sun. He still had to use tanning sprays to get some color, a fact of his genetics he believed he would have to live with for the rest of his life. He glanced over at his beautiful wife. She spent most of her time indoors, writing, but still managed a beautiful, golden tan. Not quite bronze, but a nice warm, healthy look. It went well with her now blonde hair color.

He daydreamed about the day he would play in the surf with Little Jonathan. Teaching him the mysteries of the galaxy, advanced science, throwing a frisbee, how to talk to girls. He was determined to give the boy as normal a life as he could, given Jonathan's lineage and heritage. Lo would help with that. Even if her own childhood was not exactly loving, she would show the boy how to be more ... human than he could. That adventure would begin in earnest in just a matter of weeks, but right now it's just a relaxing day next to his honey, stretched out in the Florida sunshine.

A couple of tanned, young women in scanty bathing suits walked into to the surf several dozen yards to the south of their beachfront. He subtly lowered his sunglasses to see them better. No one needed telescopic vision to appreciate the sights on this beach.

"Eyes front, mister." She didn't even lift her head from her magazine.

He grinned. "Yes, ma'am." She never let him get away with anything. Another reason he loved her so much.

*

SNEAKING OFF

He might've tried to say that he couldn't remember the circumstances under which he snuck out of the house, but that would have been lie. He had an eidetic memory. He never forgot anything. Usually a boon to his lifestyle, except when he was trying to make honest excuses.

It started innocently enough, watching the evening news. Thanks to him changing his life, he regularly ignored stories of enormous gem shipments, possible bank heists, and international coup d'etats. But even under her watchful eye, it was impossible to turn blind eye to natural disasters like earthquakes, avalanches, and even solar flares. Tonight, she was online, shopping for baby furniture, when the story broke on the national news. A hurricane had suddenly changed course and was heading right for the Florida Keys.

"Babe, I'm going to go out for a bit, get some air," he called out, heading for the door.

He made his way quickly to a nearby hangar-like building, at their private airstrip he bought without her knowledge, changed his clothes to something more appropriate, and from there, flew toward the heart of the hurricane.

Numerous well-placed super-heated explosions, air-shattering sonic booms, and artificially generated wind storms later and the hurricane diverted harmlessly out to sea.

Flying quickly back to his hidden hangar, he changed from his flight suit and ran back to their home.

She was waiting at the front door.

Arms folded. Feet apart. Toe tapping. The one eyebrow up. The right eyebrow. This was not good.

Where was an apocalypse when you needed one?

"Get enough air?" she asked cooly.

"Baby, I just—" he started.

"Don't baby me! We have a *baby* on the way and the last thing he needs is his daddy flying out in front of a hurricane doing who knows what? His LYING father, I might add."

"I didn't lie. I did get some air."

"I know. It's all over the news. A hurricane plane got video of you diverting the storm. What were you thinking?"

"I was thinking that storm was headed straight for us," he said. "You and our baby. I needed to do something. Then once I started, I started thinking about all the other people in the way of that thing that didn't have someone that could stop it, and I just had to do what I could. And you know what, honey? It felt good. Yeah, I do miss being in the spotlight, but more importantly, I miss doing *big* things. Things that only I can do."

She softened at that. He looked up and she, in her raw emotion, forgot about their cover identities and used his real name.

"I know. I was just so worried. You're not invulnerable, you know. If something would happen to you, Lex, I don't know what I would do."

***

The Other 1963
Two brothers clash in an alternate history

"Ah'm tired of lying for you, brother! No more!" stress exaggerating his New England inflection, his vowels stretching as tight as his nerves. "Ah've paid too dear a price."

His older brother bowed his well-groomed head in a way the cameras loved, then stared into his shorter sibling's blue eyes and said, "I need you here. More than ever. If Father ..."

"Father? Our dear father never intended it to be you! It was always supposed to be our brother. But when he disappointed Father by going off and getting killed, our loving father had to settle for his second choice ... you," the younger's voice colder than the November gusts outside. Invoking their late brother would rip open the old scabs, inflict the most pain. "I was never even a contender. I guess I wasn't handsome enough, tall enough ... war hero enough. Damn shame Germany and Japan had to go and surrender before I got my shot at it."

"Did Ethel put you up to ...," the older brother started.

"You leave her out of this," the younger brother's voice a low growl. "She sacrificed more than you will ever know. She raised an entire family while I was out handling your dirty

77

laundry. All these years, while I was busy with your campaigns and back-room deals and cleaning up your messes, she was raising a family a man could be proud of."

"I'm sorry. I never meant to imply that ..."

"Don't even say her name. Not with the same mouth that does who knows what to those women while your own wife is just down the hall. My wife's name doesn't come out of the same face that looks gangsters in the eye and tells them what they want to hear. The same pretty mug that lies to the American people. You will never say her name again. You hear me? Never."

"What can I do to make this right?" the elder brother asked, his tone soothing and apologetic.

"Step down," the younger sibling's voice cold and hard. "Step down and take care of your wife and children. Lord knows you've done enough. Enough for this country. Enough for the whole world. And everyone in this family has paid with their very souls to give you that chance."

"You know I can't do that," his intonation changing, strengthening, hardening with an edge he usually reserved for the military.

The argument had been brewing for ages. Tension had been building like a nor'easter, but instead of gale winds and barometric pressure, the rough seas here were triggered by unions, mob money, and repeated infidelities.

The younger of the two inseparables glared at his elder's courageous profile for a long while in the dimly lit, circular room. With a sigh of exhaustion and resignation, he lowered his slim frame into a Queen Ann arm chair, chosen specifically to keep dignitaries and underlings from getting too comfortable. In this office, everyone was an underling. In this office, it was easy to feel uncomfortable.

Looking up from the chair into his older brother's greenish gray eyes, "In three days, I'm going to announce my candidacy."

"Excellent! You'll make a great senator," the elder brother smiled, relief flooding through him. "Maybe New York. I'll come out and ..."

"I'm not going to run for Senate," the younger statesman announced quietly. "If you don't step away from this office, I'm announcing my candidacy for President of the United States."

It was the older brother's turn to go weak-kneed. A twinge of pain ran up his spine, as he lurched against the antique Resolute desk.

"You can't be serious. You don't stand a chan—" he couldn't stop himself in time.

"Don't stand a chance?" the younger man smirked. "You arrogant bastard. The sad thing is, you're probably right. I don't think anyone can run against you. They love you too much. They love her too much. You're right. I don't stand a chance. I'm not doing this to be president, you big galoot. I'm doing this to save you ... from yourself. You've done so much good, but I love you too much to sit back and watch you lose any more of your soul. This is too much power for you. It has to stop—one way or the other. I'm begging you to step away from all this."

Like dust motes in the light from the circular office's windows, a silence hung between them.

"I told you, I can't do that."

His baby brother sighed, "I know that you *won't*."

"It will tear this nation apart. You can't be serious. Do you even know how insane this sounds? It will tear our family apart!" In reality, his mind reeled with the potential impact to his administration.

"You mean the family that put a philandering pimp into this office? The same family that had an entire movie made to sensationalize you wrecking a damned boat in the war just in time to get you re-elected? That family? Well, that's the price our family will have to pay for buying our way to the top. God always demands His due, dear brother. As for tearing the nation apart, what I think you really mean is, this will tear you apart. This nation is a hell of a lot stronger than you give it credit for. I will always love you as my brother, but I hate what you are becoming."

"Pimp?"

"You're right. 'Pimp' isn't exactly accurate, unless you count your secretaries. Maybe 'John' would be a much more appropriate term," the younger brother's voice a meld of irony and accusation.

The elder brother's face froze, eyes hardening. It was the face his younger brother had seen an October ago. Back then, it was only about global destruction. Now, it was serious. It was about power. Now, it was about disappointing the family.

"You can't win," the older brother's New England accent threatening to erupt. "You're as dirty as I am. You were by my side the entire time."

"You're right. I am dirty. As dirty as you? Not even Hoover is that dirty. But I am willing to face this country, and our family, and clear my conscience. Will this great nation forgive me? Maybe not. Will the family? Never. Do I have your charisma, following, or power base? Hell no. Can I win? Definitely not. But I can split the party. I can tell the truth. Coming from me, somebody will listen. Hoover will listen. And you won't win. Not with this."

Bobby held up a worn, brown leather satchel, thrusting it into his brother's hands. "Step down now. Don't make me use this. I love you and have done everything you or this family has ever asked of me, but don't make me a blackmailer just to save you."

The older brother opens the case and pulls out some of the papers to study them.

"Where ... where did you get all this?"

"Some crazy, white-haired old man in a weird metal car showed up at the house and gave it to me. Said that if I used this, I could 'stop you.' I knew about all this before, but this is proof."

"There are photographs, dates, even films," the elder moaned. "Hoover has to be behind this. Who else could gather all this?"

"It's not Hoover. The old man gave me a file on him, too, some stuff you won't believe. Stuff that makes your antics look like child's play. Trust me, Hoover will fall in line now."

The Attorney General continued purposefully as he walked to the door, "I want you to take this case and study what's in it. Study it well, Jack. Because in it, is every dirty lie I've ever told to protect you. All the agencies and unions we've ever screwed over. All the women. All the money. Every deal you ever made to be king. You read every page and look at every photo, Jack, because everything is going to be different. Nothing will ever be the same when you get back. Nothing."

"Okay, Bobby. You win. Let's talk this over. We'll take the whole weekend, if necessary. Jackie will be disappointed, and the Secret Service will flip, but I'll cancel the Dallas trip."

***

The Truth in the Dark
(What Lies in the Dark)

Two modern tales combine the supernatural, serial killings,
and a hidden truth.

His Prey struts into the mouth of the darkened alley. It's almost cliché. He awaits in the back entrance of a closed restaurant, past the reeking dumpsters.

Shadows drape across his still form as he watches her.

The staccato of the spiked heels punctuating her shapely legs; the swish of her black miniskirt paired with a snug leather bodice. Short, fiery auburn hair tops her slender neck. Of all of her features, her neck fascinates him the most. Her attire does not interest him. After all, one doesn't concern themselves with the packaging of their food.

Earlier, he had taken the precaution of breaking the bug-speckled light bulb in the metal fixture above the doorway. After years of a nocturnal existence, he requires very little light to see. The neon from the club a block away provides his Prey enough light to navigate the alley. He watches her consider retracing her steps. The darkness and stench of rotting lettuce and seafood wafting from the dumpster may be making her skittish. He smiles in the dark as she sees the lights from the club at the far end of the alley and pushes on. It would be a shame to lose a prey due to rotten shrimp.

Covered from neck to toe by a long black coat, black T-shirt, slacks, and gloves, his pale face seems to float in the shadows. His features, mostly obscured by the collar of his coat and the brim of an old-fashioned fedora, display a preternatural calm. Beneath the hat, his blackened hair slicks back from the slight widow's peak at the center of his boyish face. Had anyone been able to see him clearly, his youthful features place him between late teens and early thirties. Damien is definitely older than he appears.

*

It is not even ten p.m., and the Prey is on her way to a nearby club that caters to the local wannabes and pretenders.

Damien himself visited this particular establishment just last weekend, slicing through the dancing throng the way a shark circles through a school of cod. He noted the number of unescorted females among the prey, how early they arrived, and what time they departed. The female prey dressed as harlots, showing not only ankle but knee and thighs nearly to their privates. The males, while more conservatively dressed, wore as much makeup, or even more, than their inappropriately dressed counterparts. All of the posers were fair-skinned, ruby-lipped, garbed in black, with nails polished deep obsidian. Piercings and tattoos, displayed proudly, were more common than watches.

While lacking in body art, Damien, too, wore black exclusively, not to be trendy or Goth, but to better stalk the night, in what he considers his personal game preserve. He glided through the crowd, as untouched by the bone-shaking thump of the bass subwoofers, as he was unseen by the clientele. When Damien found a darkened corner from which to observe, he paused his shark-like drifting. He occasionally sipped from a glass of wine. Stronger spirits burn his throat and wither his control, unleashing a more unpleasant side to his personality. Even if someone noticed him, what would they actually see? One more black-clad, faceless drone among a sea of white-faced, eye-lined imposters. Damien estimated many of the dancers were of college age.

He was all but invisible. The mere thought of any comparison to prey irritated him more than the strobing lights and the pulsing beat ever could. Looking around, he mused at how many of these self-deluded cattle consider themselves dangerous or even predators. He watched, and he hungered.

*

Tonight's Prey looks as healthy as she does haughty. Her bare arms are free of any visible needle marks. He will not risk contamination. Her hair conveys a healthy sheen. While not slender, she will never be considered obese. She is perfect for his needs.

He selected her specifically in advance, knowing this is one of the few shortcuts from the free public parking to the club. Besides the minimal lighting, he chose this particular pathway to the night spot to avoid traffic light cameras or ATM video cameras. Damien isn't terribly concerned about himself appearing on videotape, but it wouldn't do for his Prey to disappear on video.

To further confound the authorities, he never hunts in the same town where he rests during the day. This hunting ground is distant enough to divert suspicion and large enough to host a number of the clubs he uses as bait. Besides, in a city this size, no one will concern themselves over a few missing prey amongst a population of hundreds of thousands.

*

Distance becomes more critical as The Need wracking Damien grips him more often than it did in his younger years. When he Became, just before leaving university, what seems an eternity ago, he needed to feed but every few months. Now,

The Need has grown, threatening to consume him, drive him mad if he does not satisfy it. Through experimentation, he learned to preserve and stock refrigerated supplies, but even they dwindle faster than in years past.

He thinks back to the days when he first Became the creature he is now. His father couldn't understand the transformation in his son and sent him to numerous doctors and sanatoriums. None of them had been able to *cure* him of his *affliction*.

Damien refuses the pollution of television or a cellular phone in his abode, but he does partake in the riches of the Internet. Using a laptop to avail himself of a wi-fi signal near his lair, Damien keeps current on the latest techniques in modern criminology. Well aware fingerprinting has been used since the mid-1800s, gloves are mandatory. After all these years, the authorities may have his prints on file, but he learned long ago to never underestimate an opponent. Even a being such as himself must learn to adapt over time in order to elude his pursuers.

His online research includes news. The authorities discovered the bodies of several women in the region. Each cadaver displayed discolored neck wounds, suction so intense no human mouth could produce it. Puncture wounds located on the throat, the exact same distance and size every time. The media dubs them "The Dracula Killings."

*

Damien fades deeper into the shadows as his Prey passes by, unaware of his presence. He reaches out to silently render her unconscious. She struggles for a moment, and he lowers her tenderly to the rough pavement of the alley. His senses drink in the aroma of her shampoo, her perfume, her soap. He looks down on her smooth face and for a moment contemplates what it would be like to take a mate, to allow someone to truly see him, in all his dark glory. Would a beauty with skin like this ever forsake the sun? No. A mortal woman could never acknowledge the reality of his existence, let alone accept his appetites. Even if they could, sooner or later, they will age and die, or he will need to make them prey. He looks away from her face, his eyes welling with unspoken fury at the inequity of his fate.

He must carry her to his vehicle where he will transport her to his lair. Once there, he will exsanguinate her and drink his fill. The old, white van is as modest as it is unassuming. No one would give it a second glance. Even though he inherited his family's fortune, he needs to make it last for what he imagines will be a very long lifetime. A predator such as he should never have to sully himself with manual labor, so he lives as frugal a lifestyle as possible. As unmemorable as the van may be, Damien takes the precaution of cross-swapping the license plates with several white vans whose registration stickers indicate they will not renew for months. Long before the rightful owners notice the switched tags, he will swap them out several times more.

He reaches to pick up his Prey.

*

Damien's face smashes into the brick of the alley wall like a speeding car. An iron-hard hand holds him by the back of the neck, lifting him off his feet, scraping his face along the rough wall. The spent hypodermic syringe and fedora fall to the ground.

"Do you know how much trouble you are causing, boy?" a deep voice rumbles from behind him. Damien's only thoughts are the indescribable pain in his face and neck. With his face pressed sideways into the wall, he is unable to see the figure behind him.

"You have no idea at what you are playing. I have been watching you. If even *that* comes to light, it will draw more attention my way than I care for. I have spent decades crafting this persona, and frankly, I have no wish to change at this point. I am quite comfortable now. The thought of uprooting my life because some petulant youth feels the need to cosplay irritates me. You are not going to enjoy seeing me 'irritated.'"

Through the pain, and still pinned to the wall, Damien kicks backward, like a child in a temper tantrum. His kicks land solidly against his attacker's shins. Too solidly. There is no effect. The iron grip around the back of his neck doesn't waiver. The pressure holding him to the wall is machine-like in its power. No human could so effortlessly pin a full-sized adult off the ground with one hand like this. The hand that Damien could see was as white as snow.

"Even if no one discovers my personal interest, you are drawing too much attention to the truth. 'The Dracula Killings'? Could you be more obtuse? The only aspect of this whole episode that vexes me more than having to locate and deal with you is the fact a self-deluded, little brat such as yourself considers themselves a predator. You wouldn't know a predator if one bit you, which, unfortunately, I am not going to do."

Even through the pain and pressure, Damien could not withhold his shock. "You're going to let me live?"

"Do not be ridiculous. Even had you not drawn so much attention so closely to the truth, I could not possibly suffer an insult such as this charade. I have been to your 'lair' and seen the truth. You are just a sad little boy playing monster. You have no idea what a real monster is capable of."

Effortlessly, his attacker spins him around and slams his back into the wall, knocking the breath from his lungs. Shocked and gasping, Damien looks down in time to see a ghostly white hand spray pepper mist into his face. Screaming from the pain and unable to see, Damien's next sensation is being stabbed multiple times in the chest with a small knife. Unbearable pain rips through his frame as he drops to the ground like an empty sack. The last thing he sees is the blurry form planting the knife in the Prey's hand and the pepper spray being fitted into her other lifeless fist.

"A shame to waste all of this warm blood really, but finding your drained corpses would fuel the media fires and incite the police all that much more. As worthless as you were in life, your death will, at least, provide a nice misdirection. As you fade away, even a pretender such as yourself can appreciate that truth."

*

What Lies in the Dark

Death is waiting on them. Detectives Grapewin and Esteban smile at each other as they approach the crime scene. Dr. Death is not only the best in the field but a perfectionist. It is a common perception among the homicide investigators, Grapewin and Esteban are his favorites.

His real name, of course, is not Dr. Death, but Dr. Samuel Chefliu, senior medical examiner and CSU lead. He has been a medical examiner in Mecklenburg County for so long no one else even remembers his predecessor. His appearance on a scene means someone has passed beyond the mortal coil by means other than accidental. Dr. Death does not *do* accidents. His lackeys handle those. Chefliu may not be the actual personification of murder, but he is at least its personal assistant. The man knows more about inflicting death on a human body than anyone alive. A reputation Chefliu does not discourage from others perpetuating. It tends to keep subordinates quietly in line.

*

The crime scene officer logs the detectives in and hands them blue rubber gloves and booties. An anonymous call came in at 11:23 p.m. saying someone is struggling in the alley. Uniformed officers arrive at 11:45 to investigate and find two dead bodies.

*

"Yo, Senior Muerte, the tan looks good on you. I take it the Bahamas was a fun trip?" Esteban asked. Dr. Death has taken his first vacation in years.

"That's *Muerte del Médico* to you, Esteban. And I can honestly say I find my new coloration interesting. I haven't sported a tan in a very long time. I think it suits me. My time off was both rewarding and relaxing. Much of the pressure I felt prior to my sabbatical seems eased. Speaking of which, may we begin?"

"No blue gloves, Doc?" Grapewin asks.

91

Without looking at his white latex covered hands, Chefliu replies, "No. Sometimes, I prefer the old ways. The modern blue ones, I find unnatural."

"Hey, who doesn't like Smurf hands?" Esteban quips.

"Doc, would you do the honors?" Grapewin, ignoring Esteban and passing Chefliu the hand scanner.

Dr. Death himself had lobbied tirelessly with the procedural boards to ensure detectives not touch dead bodies at any crime scenes. It isn't that he doesn't trust detectives, but wants to ensure the integrity of the chain of evidence. The fewer the number of hands touching the body, the less chance of a jury's perception of mishandling, and a higher conviction rate. One of many procedural and technical changes Dr. Death had made over the years to increase the city's homicide closure rate.

He found funding, donations, and corporate sponsors to provide the homicide divisions with portable hand scanners which scan someone's fingerprints in the field, link data to VICAP and numerous other police and federal databases, and in just moments, have the identity and background of the scanned individuals. The data ports instantly to a laptop, or in this case, an iPad, carried by the investigating team.

"The young lady's name was Cynthia Durban. No wants or warrants. Student at UNCC. Led a relatively clean life. Despite her goth appearance, a good girl. Pretty rare these days," Esteban summarizes.

"Ah. Here we go. It looks as if our other DB, Mr. Damien Johnson, was a person of interest for stalking while in college. The vic, Lisa Bannister, reported it and the detectives in charge brought him in for questioning. There are hints in the report about the possibility of other stalking victims, but no one came forward. Seems the problem went away when Daddy Johnson's checkbook showed up." Esteban's scanning through the electronic report.

"Many a youth's troubles can be traced directly to overindulgent parents." Doc Chefliu comments.

"You sound like you have some firsthand knowledge, Doc?" Grapewin asks.

"Yes, I guess you could say I come from a family of some means and my parents not only indulged my excesses but encouraged them. Many a time, my family's social position enabled my somewhat petulant early life. It took me years to realize I need to live *in* this world and not above it. From that moment, I realized I needed to contribute to society, not be a drain on it. What about you, Detective Grapewin, is your badge recompense for a misspent youth?"

"Just the opposite. Kansas farm boy goes military to see the world. A hitch at Fort Bragg and a few college courses later and I am serving and protecting here in Charlotte. A few years from now, I'm eligible for my 'twenty and out.' Pretty boring stuff. Christ. I think I just depressed myself."

"Good, because you depress the rest of us all the time," his junior partner, Esteban, jibes.

*

Grapewin watches as his younger partner wanders off to see what he can find. Jorge (pronounced "George") Esteban is perhaps one of the ugliest people Grapewin has ever met. A gap in his front teeth does not complement the pushed-in face. Esteban explains it as one too many fist fights in his youth. Grapewin met the Latino's mother and knows genetics are at play. Squat and muscular, Esteban is a just a few years from getting a paunch that will slow him down. One too many churros. Esteban spent most of his youth denying his Hispanic roots, but flipped his position in the past decade, and has become a zealot about embracing his heritage. Despite his sometimes inappropriate humor, Grapewin considers Esteban one of the finest investigative minds in town.

*

"What's your take on this, Doc?" Grapewin asks, knowing damn well Dr. Death would never offer an incorrect initial assessment. It would tarnish his reputation.

93

After some thought, Chefliu stands and gestures to the bodies.

"Mind you, this assessment is at first glance, and when we get them to the lab, we might come up with completely different findings." As if. "It looks to be much as it appears. Ms. Durban was injected with a syringe containing an unknown chemical agent. You can see the puncture mark here on her neck. The syringe lays there. Trace evidence in the ampule will tell us exactly what to look for in her tox screen.

"Mr. Johnson received an ample dose of pepper spray, as evidenced by the irritation and redness around his eyes and face, and, more obviously, the empty can of spray here. Stabbed several times to the torso with the knife laying there, Mr. Johnson's COD, obviously, is the numerous puncture wounds to his chest. When he fell, he must have abraded his face on the brick wall there. We will compare the stab wounds with the blade, but there is no doubt in my mind, that is the weapon that killed Mr. Johnson. Her cause of death will likely be the injected chemical, the ensuing struggle, or both. Time of death is not really an issue. They were still fresh when we arrived on the scene. The evidence in this scene is so blatant it is nearly a waste of my time."

"So, your take is Johnson attacks her with a syringe to kill or snatch her, she fights him off with pepper spray and guts him with a knife, and they both end up cold?" Grapewin asks.

"Not at all what I said," Dr. Chefliu says coolly. "I merely present facts, it is your job to make deductions from the evidence."

*

"Esteban, what have you got?" Grapewin asks.

"Not much. I started the uni's canvassing the neighborhood, talking to everyone, looking for anything out of the usual. We are interviewing people at the club down the alley. Standard stuff. What about you?"

Grapewin summarized Chefliu's initial thoughts.

"There are a couple of pieces of physical evidence that fit his theory. Someone broke that light bulb recently. You can tell by the size of the fragments. If it had been broken a while back, the pieces would be trampled smaller. Johnson probably did it to make the alley darker," Grapewin says.

"Probably didn't want anyone to see him in that dumbass hat. I mean, who wears hats at all these days, let alone something right out of a Bogart movie?"

Grapewin thinks about the fedora. "Somebody who's trying to avoid having his picture taken by a traffic or security cam. The brim covers more than a baseball cap, and with a coat collar up, almost no part of your head, hair, or face would be visible. It's conspicuous, but all you have to do is throw it in the nearest trash container, and any witnesses would only remember the old-fashioned hat. You could walk right past them," Grapewin says. "But you're right. Wearing a hat like that says something about the wearer. Like they identified with a time long past. Doc seems to think this is an open and shut, so I doubt we'll need to get a profiler in on this, but an old fedora definitely speaks volumes about Johnson. I just don't what it's saying."

"It's saying he don't own a mirror," Esteban jokes.

*

The M.E.'s team set up lights, and the alley is brighter than noon. Dr. Death continues to preside over the area. He allows no one to collect evidence but himself to preserve the sanctity of the crime scene. Most of the cops think of him as a control freak, but none could argue his results. His case files and chains of evidence are impeccable and inarguable in court. As frustrated as the District Attorney's office may be at not getting him to appear in court, they are placated with the accuracy and thoroughness of his evidentiary data. Many a defense attorney moans when they see his name on the evidence reports.

As ironclad as his conclusions are, the good doctor never appears in court himself. He sends one of his assistant medical examiners to present his findings. "The data speaks for itself. I have no wish to be drawn into the spectacle or garishness of a trial. My time is better spent otherwise."

To ensure he is not available for trial, the head of the forensics department purposely schedules himself on the night shift. His assistants look at this policy with mixed feelings. They love they do not have to work nights, but heaven help you if you do not perform well in court, presenting his data with anything less than the reverence it deserves. Several years ago, after a case was lost due to the forensic testimony, one assistant M.E. resigned rather than face the wrath of Dr. Chefliu. He currently works as a morgue attendant at a county hospital. In another state.

*

"While you were chowing down on churros with our brothers in uniform, I found a business address for young Mr. Johnson's father and an insomniac judge to give us a warrant," Grapewin tells his partner. "Let's roll. We will take a look around first and then call in CSU to really rumble the place. Grab the video camera so we can document first entry."

"Is the churro comment a racist thing? If it's a racist thing, I need to go talk to my amigos down in HR," Esteban said.

"Do you, or do you not, like churros?"

"You don't see me busting on you about donuts, do you?"

"I like donuts," Grapewin replies. "Got nothing to do with being white. Donuts are a cop thing, and if you ever become a real cop, you will figure that out. So, churros?"

"Yeah. They were awesome, but those uni's are pigs, man. I brought a whole bag from this place I know, and they ate nearly all of them."

"So besides epicurean reviews, did our amigos in uniform have anything to add to the actual case?" Grapewin asks.

"They interviewed the kids all night from the club down the alley and no one, including the doormen, remembered ever seeing our boy. In their defense, though, hundreds of people pass through that door each night. Unless he was wearing that stupid hat, he would fit right in. All pasty white faces and black clothes. It's like Disco of the Living Dead."

*

The car pulls to a stop in front of an abandoned medical supply warehouse.

"J and J Medical Wholesalers. That's the company that registered the van according to the VIN numbers," Esteban says.

Grapewin looks across the seat at his partner. "What van?"

"Did I not mention the van?"

"No, dumbass, you were busy casting aspersions about my diversity sensitivity."

"I wasn't casting you in any part—" Esteban begins.

"WHAT VAN?" Grapewin likes his partner, but Esteban's about a half step away from Grapewin's last nerve.

"The uni's found an old white, POS Econoline Ford not too far from the scene. Stolen plates, but when they ran the VIN, it came up with a registration to J and J Medical Wholesalers," Esteban explains. "Damien's dear old dad owned J and J Medical Wholesalers. He kicked the bucket under some highly questionable circumstances. Fedora Boy inherited and liquidated everything but the van and the warehouse."

"Do you think you might want to lead with that the next time instead of dead-end interviews?"

"We called in one of Dr. Death's boys, Jaidan, I think was the one, to process the van. The tall one." Grapewin's glare pushes Esteban to move it along. "Anyway, no prints inside, but some zip ties, a ball gag, and a few movers' blankets. Practically a Do-It-Yourself Snatch Kit. We're certain this was what Fedora Boy was planning on transporting the vic in.

Jaidan found a few hairs that could be possible matches to some of the vics in the Dracula Killer thing."

"So, you're just now getting around to telling me about the possible connection and address to our deceased suspect and some statewide serial killings?" Grapewin asks incredulously.

"You know, Grape, you get a little cranky when you don't get your morning donut."

*

Grapewin gets out of the unmarked car, pops the trunk and removes a formidable pair of bolt cutters.

"You keep the Jolly Green Giant's nail clippers in your trunk?" Esteban asks.

"Doesn't everyone?"

After cutting the padlock from the garage style door and rolling it up, the two detectives step inside, pulling on blue latex gloves.

Grapewin looks at the rolling garage door. "I bet you could probably drive an old Ford Econoline right in here to unload a body unseen," he says, glaring at his partner.

Esteban clicks the light switch. It takes a moment for the fluorescents to flicker on as if rarely used. "No windows. No natural light. Bad Fang-Shui."

"It's pronounced 'fungshway.' But you're not wrong. Feng-shui is about architectural goodness, and goodness has nothing to do with this place," Grapewin says, motioning to a slightly inverted autopsy table in the middle of the room, a strange vacuum-like device near the table, and an old refrigerator off to the side. "Smells like a butcher shop in here. Keep videoing this stuff."

"Yeah, no shit. This had to be his *kill room*. Esteban aims the small video camera at a corrugated plastic hose connected to a modified vacuum pump. The hose ended with a rubber seal and two sharp syringe-like needles in the middle. "A thing like this, combined with a tilted autopsy table, might be able to suck all the blood out of a body pretty quickly."

"Esteban, you ever see an autopsy table with restraints on it before?" Grapewin asks.

*

The CSU team catalogs and bags everything. Grapewin and Esteban find six pints of blood plasma in the refrigerator and a variety of injectable narcotics. Most of which are what you might inject into someone to render them unconscious but leave the system quickly, dissipating and undetectable. A laptop rests on the workbench. By the time they get to the back of the warehouse, Grapewin is not even surprised to find the polished mahogany coffin. He is, however, a little shocked at the map pinned up over the workbench wall.

"How stupid and cliché was this guy? It looks like he has red push pins in the map for where he abducted those girls and blue ones for where he dumped the bodies. If he were alive, we wouldn't even need a confession," Esteban says.

Grapewin studies the map. "Uh, Jorge, there are more pins than we have victims. How many girls did this asshole kill? We need to get uniforms to the locations of those extra blue pins and see if there are bodies there."

"Hey, I'm right about another thing," Esteban says, looking around. "No mirrors."

*

Grapewin and Esteban arrive at the M.E.'s office that evening a little ahead of schedule. They step into Dr. Chefliu's private office, just as he closes a desk drawer.

"Ah, gentlemen, prompt as usual. Excellent. I, and my team, processed the evidence collected so far, most expeditiously. I think we have a few findings which may interest you," Dr. Chefliu says.

"Well, Doc, we'll take whatever you've got, but so far, this is just like you said, a slam dunk," Esteban replies, sitting on the only stool in the room, while Grapewin leans on the edge of the desk.

"I seriously doubt I have ever used the expression 'slam dunk' in my entire existence, Detective Esteban. That being said, we did uncover some facts supporting my initial assumptions. Traces in the syringe and Ms. Durban's blood are a confirmed narcotic. If administered in the right dose, it would have rendered her unconscious, or at least very malleable. The full tox screen will be forthcoming, but since we had the syringe, the lab was able to test quickly for a specific substance. The syringe itself bears no prints whatsoever. Mr. Johnson was wearing gloves, so the total lack of prints further implicates him, even if indirectly. Ms. Durban's prints are the only ones on the pepper spray and knife.

"Jaidan positively matched hair, fibers, even paint particulates from the van, to a number of unsolved murders. Combined with the deluge of evidence found at the warehouse and it appears as if you may have closed what the press has so ridiculously dubbed *The Dracula Killings*," Chefliu states, standing somewhat stooped near the darkened window, his white hair in stark contrast to his newly tanned face.

"Speaking of which," he continues with his lecture, "even with the other bodies' decapitated state, we were able to match the marks on their throats with the suction device you found.

"Mr. Johnson used his device to exsanguinate them, harvesting the blood you found in the refrigerator. We also matched that to the other victims. Either as anticipating an insanity defense or part of a genuine psychosis, he decapitated them and drove a wooden stake into their remains. There was nothing supernatural about him. Just a self-deluded young man."

"Pretty much wraps it up as far as we're concerned. Email us your report when you have it finalized, Doc," Grapewin says as he stands. "I think we are gonna tie a bow on it and toss it in the closed pile. The chief will make a statement to the press about how CMPD wrapped up The Dracula Killings through tireless police work, when it was really some college girl with a can of pepper spray and a folding knife. Either way, we're on to the next one."

"Contact my office if you have any questions about the data," Chefliu says, opening the door for the detectives. "We live to serve."

"Doc, if I didn't know better, I would say that was almost sarcasm," Esteban says.

"Detective Esteban, sarcasm is commonly hostility disguised as humor. I believe the word you were looking for is irony."

*

Chefliu stands at the door in thought for a few seconds after the detectives leave. Unconsciously, his posture straightens to his full height. Sitting at the desk, he opens the desk drawer, pulling out a business card and a burner phone.

"All Night Spray Tans? I want to confirm you will be open later this evening and make an appointment if so. Name? Make the appointment under Grapewin. Nine-thirty should be fine. Thank you, I will see you then."

Chefliu glances at the institutional clock on the wall. He puts the business card and phone back in the drawer, behind a plastic box of colorful stick pins and white vinyl gloves. Nine-thirty will give him just enough time to have a quick meal and make the drive. There will be plenty of time when he gets back to type his report.

All will be as it should, as long as he moves the two new body bags down to the incinerator before daylight.

***

Cancer-Free

Aliens can rid us of cancer, one way or the other

"When something seems too good to be true—"

"A pessimist comes along and ruins it for everyone," Jeremy's lab assistant, Dell, snarked.

"When something seems too good to be true," Jeremy repeated, "it probably is."

"Doc, what could possibly be bad about aliens that have come to Earth to remove all our cancer?" Dell asked.

"I don't know, Dell, but that doesn't mean there isn't ... something."

"I admire the hell out of you, Doc, but at times," Dell told his mentor, "you can be a real buzz kill."

"Yeah, like I haven't heard that ... today," Dr. Jeremy Hamilton said. It may be true. Hamilton's friends, colleagues, students, and ex-wife had all made a point of his cynical nature at one time or another. His ex-wife had said that he was living proof God had a sense of humor to put such a pessimistic personality in a ruggedly good-looking, intelligent, specimen. That was shortly before she left him to live with a physics professor tenured at the same university. *It's not the size of the ship, but the motion of the subatomic particles in quantum flux.* She claimed it was Hamilton's sardonic nature to cause her to nickname him "Eeyore." He called her "Polly." Her name was Allison. She never really connected, or appreciated, the Pollyanna reference.

The aliens had appeared several weeks ago, announcing their good intentions in all languages. In the U.S., a drone ship landed on the White House lawn. In other countries, they landed at the residences of their respective leaders. They claimed they came in peace. To demonstrate their benevolence, they proposed that they would effectively remove all the cancer cells from human bodies. They suggested Earth send a delegation to interview and investigate their claims.

An enormous starship hovered in geosynchronous orbit around the globe. Ironically, their ship wasn't shaped so much like a saucer as a large crystal pyramid. While the ship seemed to be crystalline, it was both clear and opaque at the same time. Another mystery needing solved. The extraterrestrials offered very little data on their systems. If they were friendly, why not share their technology?

"If not to help us," Dell asked, "why DO you think they came here?"

"Just because we don't know the answer right now," Jeremy answered, "doesn't mean there isn't one. Or the one they so readily provided."

"Well, what I know, is that if they do what they say they are going to do, you are going to be out of business," Dell said, "and I picked a horrible field."

Again, Jeremy had to admit that his assistant was not wrong. As one of the leading oncology researchers at the university, the eradication of cancer would leave him adrift and make Dell's selected career path ill-chosen. Jeremy hoped that the alien's claims were true. He had lost his mother at an early age to cervical cancer and his father to prostate cancer. Two more reasons he had chosen the path he had. He hoped to help eliminate cancer in his lifetime. Now that all seemed irrelevant.

"Dell, I don't know what their real motives are, but nobody, not even little green men, travel across the universe out of the goodness of their hearts, no matter how many they may have," Jeremy stated, looking out the window of his lab. "Let's find out why they did."

*

"We have an application from one Dr. Jeremy Hamilton," the committee chairman said, as he passed around copies of Hamilton's dossier. "The good doctor has impeccable credentials, St. Jude's, Mayo, and currently at Princeton. While not yet tenured, he has done well for himself, making several minor breakthroughs in carcinoma metastases and then in neoplasia growth inhibitors, whatever those may be. He teaches and researches at Princeton while regularly making rounds at the Princeton Cancer Center."

A dozen men and women the president hand-picked and United Nations approved, gathered to choose a select team to interact with the aliens and investigate their proposed methods for eradicating cancer. Since the aliens' arrival and suggestion for an investigative envoy, applications and resumes of those wanting to meet the newcomers inundated governments around the world. The committee ranged from esteemed medical research professionals to accomplished political operators to intelligence officers. They were evaluating possible applicants from the thousands of candidates who volunteered to interact with the extraterrestrials. The powers that be tasked the committee with selecting a small team consisting of a medical researcher, a security analyst, and a diplomat.

"Especially for such a young man," said one of the elder committee members, best known for his political aspirations and manipulations. "Why hasn't he tenured or moved higher in his field?"

The chairman flipped through Jeremy's folder, finally stopping toward the end. "It seems while academically astute and one heckuva researcher, our good Dr. Hamilton has himself a bit of an attitude problem."

"What kind of attitude?"

A committee member from a leading intelligence agency picked up a different folder.

"It seems the good doctor is a bit of skeptic. He spends as much time disproving others' findings as he does generating new ones for himself. He values the truth above all else, no matter who it hurts. He's not very popular amongst his peers because of it and even his superiors are put off a bit by his cynical attitude and personality."

The chairman eyed the intelligence folder from the end of the table. "Is he any kind of security risk?"

The intelligence officer looked at the folder a bit more and glanced up. "Just the opposite, actually. The ex-wife has her own income, resources, and romantic interest with a physics professor at the same school. Despite that, the divorce seems mutual and amicable. No debts to speak of, no affairs, no gambling issues or vulnerabilities that we can find. Seems like the doc is clean. And more importantly, incorruptible."

The elder committee member spoke again, "What about this penchant for cynicism? Do we really want to send a 'Debbie Downer' on a mission to establish diplomatic relations with our first contact with an extraterrestrial race? Don't we want things to go as smoothly as possible?"

"He does seem the sort to muddy the water wherever he goes," the chairman added.

The intelligence officer looked at each man, one at a time, with each sentence.

"Gentlemen, Dr. Hamilton doesn't care about politics. He doesn't care about popularity. He doesn't care about any single person. He only cares about ending cancer and the truth. He can't be bought, blackmailed, or dissuaded. I couldn't pick a better candidate. Worst-case scenario, we *take* the anti-cancer technology from E.T. And if Hamilton muddies the water a bit, well, it's still wet. You never know. He may drown himself in it."

*

Dr. Jeremy Hamilton, now approved to be a part of the Extraterrestrial Integration Operation (E.I.O. - governments love their acronyms!) possessed two first-class airline tickets and a car sent to deliver him and his assistant to the rendezvous point. For security's sake, the intelligence agencies involved selected mid-state Kansas as the initial meeting point between the extraterrestrials and the E.I.O. The car drove Jeremy and Dell to a private airfield in Kansas City, where a military helicopter picked them up to deliver the scientists to a barren spot about seventy miles northwest of Topeka.

Jeremy stepped out of the darkened SUV into the middle of the hastily established Forward Operating Base (F.O.B.). Squinting in the harsh summer sunlight, Jeremy took in the immense temporary Quonset huts and military presence.

Not exactly diplomatic and welcoming, Hamilton thought, as he scanned the heavy artillery and personnel carriers. Automatic rifles and camouflaged BDUs were everywhere. *Perhaps not unwarranted. Evidently, I am not the only one with reservations about our new friends. But then again ...*

"You think this all here to defend us against them if it goes pear-shaped?" Dell asked.

Looking around at all the military presence, now noting a lack of anti-aircraft weapons and missiles. "No. I think this is to keep *us* in line."

"Dr. Hamilton?" an officer greeted them and extended his hand. "I am Major Vincenzo. I will be your liaison officer. If you need anything, please let me know, and I will see what we can do. I'll give you a quick rundown. You will be part of the first three-person team to interact with the extraterrestrials. They picked the number. We wanted more, but they insisted. Your assistant will have to remain here and help organize your

107

data and reports in your absence. The extraterrestrials will transport you and your fellow delegates to their main ship above the U.S. where you will talk with them about their science and diplomatic relations with Earth."

"Is E.T. going to shuttle or beam them up?" Dell asked with a smile.

"Yes," the major said. "When we asked, we were told 'both.' Before they are shuttled to the main ship, they'll be 'beamed up' part of the way. Another technology we would love to know about."

"Roddenberry would be so proud," Dell joked.

A craft floated directly over the base. Just like the White House craft, it appeared to be a crystalline pyramid with each side of the base about sixty feet wide.

"Looks like your ride is here, Doc," Dell said.

"I haven't had time to gather equipment, recording gear—" Hamilton stammered at the sight of the glass-like ship.

"We didn't have an ETA on when they would come," Major Vincenzo explained, looking up at the floating vessel. "Seems like it's right now. I wouldn't worry, Doc. I seriously doubt they plan to kill us three geeks at a time."

But Dr. Hamilton was already gone.

*

The three delegates stood in a large room in the center of the pyramid. The walls were transparent and they watched as the world sped away. There was no sense of movement inside the craft.

"What's going—"

"We apologize for the suddenness of your transportation," a deep baritone voice echoed in the room. "We will be arriving at the prime craft in moments. Please be patient."

Hamilton moved to the edge of the room, watching the pyramidal shuttle rise farther and farther from the Earth below. *We're not in Kansas anymore, Toto.*

*

The crystalline pyramid that carried the delegation rose to meet a much larger version of the pyramidal ship. Much larger. About a thousand times larger. The shuttle craft slid easily into a relatively small square hole in the bottom of the larger ship.

Hamilton's eyes never left the wall which was now whitely opaque. Two other delegates seemed to stand next to him without his noticing. Jeremy glanced to either side to see himself flanked by a serious looking, dark-skinned woman, about his age, of African descent, and an older, well-dressed man with a slight paunch and receding hairline.

Just as they had at the F.O.B., the delegates instantaneously and suddenly blinked out of existence, only to appear somewhere else on the ship.

Hamilton and his two teammates found themselves standing in a slightly smaller room identical to the one they had just occupied. They might not have noticed the difference, but the opaque walls were suddenly closer.

Three humanoid shapes slowly faded into view. *It's like they're slowly coming into focus.* The new trio varied widely in appearance, but all wore a high-collared, knee-length, frock-like uniform, similar to an Earth priest's, but all white. White slacks and shoes completed the uniforms. Standing in the white light of the alien craft, they seemed almost ephemeral. All of the aliens were extremely human in appearance, but with a skin tone and characteristics that defied identifying a race or nationality. That is where the similarities ended.

The first member of the alien team was the tallest, at Jeremy's height. Clearly male, with a V-shaped torso, flat stomach, broad shoulders, and short dark hair that topped an inhumanly attractive face. The second was female, not just feminine, but the most beautiful woman Jeremy had ever seen. She seemed young without any signs of aging. With blondish brown hair and dark, slightly Asiatic features, she appeared both exotic, mysterious, and approachable at the same time. The third humanoid was androgynous. Neither overtly male or female, but completely bald with petite features and a slender build. The frock on the androgynous entity made it impossible to discern a male or female body type. Jeremy's eyes immediately jumped back to the female alien. *No problem discerning a body gender there. That frock is a tad snug in all the right areas.* She and the first alien were so attractive, they could easily be models. The third was so neutral as to be almost immediately forgettable.

"Greetings people of Earth," the male alien's voice was the same rich baritone they had heard earlier and without a hint of sarcasm. "We welcome you in the spirit of sharing and peace."

"Hello. I am—" Jeremy began.

"Dr. Jeremy Jefferson Hamilton," the female alien interrupted, her voice as soft as a flower petal, while looking him straight in the eye. "Your governments provided brief dossiers on each of you, so we familiarized ourselves with your credentials, but not your interests, and as you learn about us, we would also like to learn about you, personally."

Personally? I wonder how she meant that?

"Dr. Nadaya T'doyo and Dr. Duncan Nelson," the androgynous alien said looking at Jeremy's teammates.

They're BOTH doctors? I guess that makes sense. If you've got to send people to meet space aliens, may as well make them Ph.D.s.

"And what are your names, if we may ask?" Nelson asked, his British accent apparent, directing his question to the male alien.

"Unfortunately, our true designations are not pronounceable to you. For the sake of simplicity and diplomatic expediency, you may refer to me as Alpha," the male alien stated authoritatively. "Refer to my colleagues as Beta," the female nodded, "and Delta." The androgynous alien lifted its chin. "I assure you this has no bearing on rank, gender, or preference. We have simply chosen designations easy for you to remember and universal to your life experiences."

"We are very familiar with your world, cultures, languages, and technology," Delta said coolly. "We have made no secret of the fact that we have been studying your planet for some time, prior to our recent contact."

"Our goal here is to make you comfortable with us, so that we can be friends," Beta said, again looking directly at Jeremy.

"All well and good, but I have a question before we even get started," Nelson said. "If you can transport matter, why did we come up in a ... shuttle craft, I guess you would call it?"

Hmmm. Seems like the kind of question an intelligence officer would ask. Sussing out their technological limits right off the bat.

"Our matter transference systems have a very limited range," Alpha replied frankly. "The closer they operate, the more precise their accuracy. From above your base of operations, it was a safe and simple procedure to exchange an equal mass of oxygen/nitrogen mixture for your mass. Transfer from our sub-craft to our prime-craft is much more accurate. To minimize our personal contact with your general populace, we thought it best if you transferred first to our shuttle."

"Interesting," Dr. T'doyo spoke for the first time, her voice carried an almost musical lilt. "You must have to exchange like masses or the instantaneous absence would cause a popping vacuum, while the simultaneous insertion of too much matter would cause intense pressurization. Is this done on the atomic level?" directing her question to Delta, *sounding more like a physicist than a diplomat.*

"On the quantum level," the androgynous alien said, "but the negative effects would be felt on the atomic and macro levels."

"Perhaps we could relocate our discussions to someplace more comfortable for you?" Beta asked, turning with a gesture to indicate a doorway that wasn't there previously.

What could possibly be more comfortable than discussing quantum mechanics with a beautiful alien in a crystal pyramid starship thousands of miles above the Earth? Well, I could think of maybe one or two things.

*

"I find it interesting that they separated us even more," Dr. T'doyo stated when the three delegates were later alone.

"It was likely more efficient to allow us to focus on our individual interests independently," Dr. Nelson said.

"Yes, there was no possible way it could be 'divide and conquer,'" Hamilton murmured to himself. T'doyo shot him a sideways glance.

After the initial meeting and the delegates sat more comfortably, the group spent considerable time reviewing the ground rules and parameters for the meeting. The delegates made a point not to refer to it as an investigation. From there, the aliens each accompanied a delegate to specific areas of interest. Alpha directed Dr. Nelson, T'doyo left the room with the androgynous Delta, and the beautiful Beta lead Hamilton to the medical bays. Jeremy expected Nelson to object to the pairings, but the Brit cheerfully followed Alpha down the hall. The feminine alien mesmerized Hamilton. He couldn't help it. *Ironically, that nearly shapeless frock makes her even sexier than a form-fitting uniform. I have GOT to focus on the investigation.*

After the tour, the three delegates returned to a small (again crystalline, but opaque) conference room to confer. The conference room seemed somehow recently tailored and configured just for the delegates. As with every space they had been in previously, intense white light seemed to emanate from slots in the ceiling.

"Did either of you gentlemen learn anything new about our hosts?" Dr. T'doyo asked as they sat at the table.

"I say, do you think they are monitoring this room?" Dr. Nelson asked his companions as he looked around.

That is exactly what an intelligence officer would think.

"Very likely. Be mindful," Dr. T'doyo glanced around at the featureless room. Besides the crystal table and chairs, there was nothing else in the small space except a bowl of various types of fruit and a carafe of water and three glasses. Crystal, of course. A quick investigation revealed that a second door led to very human restroom facilities. They were allowed to use a simple panel on the wall to communicate with their superiors.

"Not much new to tell. The technology they will use to remove the cancer is similar to their matter transport system," Hamilton reported. "They perform full body scans on individuals to detect the cancer cells with a hand-held device. Then in a different device, somewhat similar to an open MRI bed, they swap the cancer cells out for an appropriate substitute using their matter transference tech at close range."

"Appropriate substitute?" asked Dr. T'doyo, her soft, lilting voice tinged with concern.

"Yes," Jeremy explained. "Evidently for them, that is the difficult and most time-consuming part. And by time consuming, I mean a couple of seconds. The machine's computer figures what could be safely exchanged into the affected areas of the specific patient. Sometimes, it may be a saline solution, sometimes plasma, or it can be a gelatinous protein substance we have no equivalent for, that the body will eventually assimilate. As we discussed, they just can't 'beam' the cancer cells out or the sudden vacuum created in the body would be disastrous."

"Did you learn anything about this matter transfer technology they use for the process?" Dr. T'doyo asked.

"That's the thing," Hamilton said. "They are very open about *what* they are doing, but very evasive about *how*.

"I fear I fared no better than Dr. Hamilton. The *why* to their purpose is also no clearer than when we began," Nelson interjected. "For all intents and purposes, they are using their cancer-eliminating procedure as a gesture of goodwill and to demonstrate their friendly intentions."

"Or so they claim," Jeremy stated.

"Claim?" Dr. T'doyo asked.

"I just find it hard to believe that an advanced extraterrestrial species would travel all this way to eliminate one of the banes of our existence just to meet new buddies," Hamilton frowned as he echoed a sentiment he had proposed to Dell earlier.

"Perhaps their intentions are exactly as they claim," T'doyo offered. "Maybe they are just trying to be good neighbors."

"Or ... cure a world's cancer once, that world owes you, and is at your mercy," Hamilton hypothesized. "Teach them the cure and they are set for life."

Nelson smiled. "Reminds me of an old saying: Build a man a fire and he is warm for a night. Set a man on fire and he is warm for the rest of his life." Neither of his companions seemed amused.

"Can I ask you two a personal question?" Hamilton looked at his companions. "Did you think that two of our hosts seemed naturally ... beautiful? Especially Beta."

"I would not have brought it up, but, yes." Nelson's eyes seem to defocus as he smiled and pictured the aliens. "I found Alpha, in particular, disturbingly flawless."

"Actually, Dr. Hamilton," T'doyo's said, "all three aliens were nearly perfect. As if designed to appeal to a specific gender preference. Delta would appeal to a person identifying as bisexual ... or at best, undecided."

"Perhaps their race genetically altered itself to remove all the 'ugly' genes," Nelson said.

"Maybe it was just me, but I found it particularly difficult to focus on their science while distracted by Beta," Hamilton said. Dr. T'doyo stared at him and Nelson for a long minute.

"Dr. Nelson, please feel free not answer this question if it makes you uncomfortable, but there is a reason I ask," T'doyo started. "Are you attracted to Alpha?"

"Wha—" Hamilton exclaimed. "Actually, Dr. T'doyo, I am. Very much so. Why do you ask and how did you come to that conclusion?" Nelson said. "Was there something in my manner that gave it away? In my line of work, I try very hard to be unreadable."

"No, you are fine, Dr. Nelson," T'doyo explained. "I just made a logical guess. I, myself, am attracted to Delta." The two men could barely contain their shock. "Dr. Hamilton is correct. They are very distracting. Almost intentionally so. It's something I myself would have done."

The two men looked shocked at the dark-skinned woman.

Jeremy, still reeling over the revelations of the sexual preferences of his companions, looked to T'doyo. "Why would a diplomat want to distract investigators with members of the opposite sex?"

"I can't speculate what a diplomat would want to do, Dr. Hamilton," T'doyo said frankly. "I am an intelligence operative. Dr. Nelson's orientation was in my private briefing packet."

*

The committee reconvened to discuss the initial report from the delegates. After the chairman called the room to order, the senior intelligence officer stood to address the committee. After reading from a rather sterile report of the facts, he looked at the group of politicians, doctors, and intelligence officers and provided his own insights.

"It seems our visitors are very smart. They separated our delegates and gave them tours of their ship, going into great detail about *what* they would do to show their friendly intentions, but being very evasive about *how*. They gave us practically no information about their teleportation or cancer-eliminating technology except to describe it in its most general terms. Nothing at all about their propulsion or weapons systems. They have shed no light on why they are being so magnanimous. In short, this was a very elaborate dog-and-pony show."

"What about Dr. Hamilton?" asked the chairman. "How is he performing? He was the wildcard in our selection."

"Actually, T'doyo reports that Hamilton is exceeding our expectations. He can sense something is amiss. He is the one who first vocalized that the aliens are not very forthcoming about the specifics of their technology. He also noticed something about their thought processes concerning their own personnel. It seems our galactic neighbors have specifically chosen representatives that are sexually appealing to our delegates in an attempt to distract them or even turn them. It is exactly what we would do in their shoes.

"Dr. Hamilton was also the one to point out about how little actual technology the aliens are divulging," the senior intelligence officer continued.

"The aliens ain't suspicious or on guard or anything, are they?" the chairman asked.

"It seems quite the contrary," the intelligence man replied. "According to our operative, the aliens act as if their seduction technique is working on Dr. Hamilton even more so than the others. Despite the great possibility that the delegates discussed all this in an insecure room, the visitors are continuing to move forward with that strategy."

"Is young Dr. Hamilton falling for it? Your earlier dossier on him said it's been some time since he was ... er ... in a relationship and may be primed for feminine attention."

"I don't believe that to be the case. If there is one thing the good doctor possesses more than a healthy, if somewhat neglected libido, is an obsessive dedication to the truth. The man not only cannot lie, but the very thought of it goes against his entire personality. Given that he knows nothing of strategic value and his naturally skeptical nature, I maintain we couldn't have picked a better delegate. He is utterly believable because he is utterly honest."

*

An hour later, the door to the conference room opened with the trio of aliens focusing into view just outside. Mindful of the delegates' earlier discussion, it was much easier for

Jeremy to stay focused on the investigation and not his hostess's physical charms. But upon closer observation, Jeremy could now detect tiny laugh lines around her eyes and the faintest of smile creases in her face. When able to study her discreetly, he noticed a very small beauty mark near her jawline.

I know that wasn't there before.

These new 'defects' in her appearance were subliminally subtle and made him more at ease with Beta's appearance, not less. Her beauty could still be distracting, but those little imperfections made her seem more *real*, even sexier.

Wait! What am I thinking? Those things weren't there before. They must have listened to our conversations and made adjustments to make our hosts more human to us, to put us more at ease. That's not special effects makeup. How could they have made those changes so fast?

The other two delegates were led away to continue their tour and Beta brought Jeremy back to the medical bay.

"We have decided that the best way to allay your fears about our procedures is to demonstrate its effectiveness," the beautiful alien said. She indicated the scanner laying on a crystalline work table.

"You may take this device and use it to detect carcinogenic cells on your own, so that we may remove them as a demonstration."

The device on the table had a white handle, much like a pistol grip, topped with a small, smooth-edged white box. Mounted on that, a see-through screen approximately six inches wide by four inches tall, completed the device.

"We have modified it for human usage," Beta explained. "The screen provides both easy to understand instructions as well as interactive diagnostics."

"You know that we can't provide humans for trials without first doing tests on animals, right?" Hamilton asked his host.

"We assumed as much. It is your nature," Beta acknowledged. "We calibrated the device for any biological entity, and it will detect a wide variety of physical imperfections and maladies."

Unbelievable! This device is a godsend! A hand-held scanner that can detect any disease? And she's just giving it to me? This will change medicine forever.

As Jeremy picked up the device, it activated. Holding it out in front of him, he pointed it all around the room, adjusting various settings on the screen.

"There are restrictions however," Beta warned. "We have created this specifically for you, personally, to use. Any attempt to x-ray or dismantle the device will cause it to self-destruct. This is for your own protection. Until mankind is ready, it would not be beneficial for it to reverse engineer advanced technology."

Jeremy looked down at the floor briefly. That was the first thought that had crossed his mind. How could humanity duplicate this technology to advance human medicine? His shame was quickly replaced by curiosity. *Would you look at that?*

"The device will cease to function and self-destruct after three of your days," Beta advised. "We hope that will be sufficient time to gain your trust."

"We appreciate your concerns and will bring up lab animals by tomorrow so that you can show us how your procedure works." Hamilton looked down at the scanner.

And I know just where to test this next.

*

The aliens returned the delegates to the F.O.B. the same way they left. A brief shuttle ride followed by an instantaneous popping out of, and into, existence. Teams of experts in their respective fields debriefed the delegates. Hudson deferred much of his debriefing brusquely.

"I'll get you full report as soon as I can, but right now, I only have three days to use this machine, do a thousand tests, find test subjects, and return to the ship for a demonstration of the procedure, so excuse me if I don't have time to sit around and talk about what happened."

"But Dr. Hudson—" Major Vincenzo began.

"Not now Major," Hudson said, standing and moving toward the door of the Quonset hut. "My fellow delegates can answer many of your questions. Now if you will just point us in the direction of a lab in all this, I would greatly appreciate it."

Major Vincenzo looked helplessly at Dell.

"What can I say Vinny?" Dell said with a smile. "I may be out of work soon, but till then, I'm gonna stick with the smartest guy in the room."

*

"Dell, I need you to round up as many test subjects as possible. Animal and human. Both healthy and with late stages. Get the major to fly them out here yesterday. I want all their medical records. Get us some lab assistance. Once the subjects are here, I want them to undergo every test possible to verify their conditions so we can compare it to what this thing says."

"What are you gonna be doin', Doc?" Dell asked.

Hamilton held up the scanning device. "I'm going to do some further testing and make sure I'm reading this right."

*

The man on the alien bed looked like a desiccated mummy. The white light from the alien ceiling emphasized his gaunt features even more. Jeremy looked down at him and squeezed his hand.

"Don't worry, this won't hurt a bit, Mr. Moore," Jeremy soothed the man. "They're will be some slight tingling for a minute or two and that's it."

"Then I'll be good as new, Dr. Hamilton?" Keith Moore asked weakly.

"No. I'm not going to lie to you. If everything goes as planned, this procedure removes the cancer cells, but your body will have to rebuild itself. It's suffered through quite an ordeal. It may take a long time to regain your strength and health, but the good news is: you'll have a long time to do it."

"Well, at least I'll still have my hair," Mr. Moore joked as he rubbed an emaciated hand over his bald pate. His once-thick mane destroyed by chemotherapy.

"Sit tight while I go check on some last-minute details," Jeremy said as he squeezed the man's hand. Mr. Moore looked as if he hadn't eaten in months. He barely cast a shadow on the alien bed. Skin stretched tight over emaciated muscles, the man on the bed looked more like a reject from a zombie movie than a man Jeremy's age. The chemo and radiation had done as much damage as the cancerous cells eating away at his lymphatic system. If this didn't work, Mr. Moore's ... Keith's ... remaining time could be measured in days, not years. Certainly not decades. His quality of life would be measured by the amount of agony he could endure. Jeremy prayed that the procedure worked.

At Jeremy's insistence, Dell accompanied him to the alien ship to assist with the work. Reluctant to let more humans access to their prime vessel, the aliens installed the necessary equipment aboard their shuttle and all of the work would be conducted there. After Hudson the approved the process, shuttles, carrying the equipment, would transfer the cancerous cells out of humans across the world. Once aboard, the gawking Dell was speechless for several minutes after first seeing Beta.

The animal testing of the alien cancer removal procedure worked flawlessly. Jeremy would like to have more time, years really, to observe the mice and other mammals for side effects of the alien tech that replaced their cancer cells. But they didn't have that much time. As assured by Beta, the animals seemed to experience no pain during the procedure and immediately began to show improvement. In a few days, Jeremy and Dell, under the watchful eye of the beautiful Beta, had "cured" hundreds of mice and even chimpanzees of life-threatening cancer. The aliens seemed patient and even understanding of the human need to test the procedure on as many animals as possible before human trials. He and Dell dissected random animals to make sure that the treatment eradicated all traces of cancer. The alien scanner confirmed their results. Jeremy presented his research, albeit rushed, to the E.I.O., the FDA, AMA, and the White House. Ultimately, it was the White House that overrode the others to allow Dr. Hamilton to begin human trials. Keith Moore had been selected the first among the thousands of volunteers and signed enough hold harmless waivers to fill a file cabinet. He declined having a lawyer look at them first.

"What are my choices? Sign these here papers or die? No, no. Please. Let's haggle over details for a few more months. Gimme that damned pen."

A few hours later, his white blood cell count and MRIs confirmed what the alien scanner reported. Keith Moore was the first human completely cured of cancer.

*

In a conference room identical to the one on the main ship, Jeremy slouched in a chair while Dell laid on the floor with his hands shading his eyes from the light pouring from the ceiling. Beta stood several yards away.

"Do you know what we just did?" Dell moaned.

"Yes," Jeremy answered. "I believe we just saved a man's life."

"No. No. No. If you jerk a guy from in front of a bus, THAT saves a man's life," Dell's hand still covered his eyes. "Do you know what we just did? We cured fragging cancer. Not just put it in remission, but fragging CURED it."

"No. You did not," Beta said impassively.

"Whoa there, Carmen Elektra!" Dell was sitting straight up now. "There's a guy on a bed not five yards from here who could live another fifty years. A few hours ago his ticket was scheduled to be punched before we flip the calendar at the end of the month. My guess is: he's calling it cured."

"No, she's right," Jeremy said flatly. He looked like he had just seen ghost. "We didn't *cure* cancer. We just transferred it. Where did we transfer it to, Beta?"

Beta was already fading from view.

*

Jeremy and Dell continued to operate the machine on numerous volunteers. Each seemed to undergo a miraculous change in health. Each patient now seemingly cancer-free. The alien matter transference tech beamed the processed cancer patients to a hospital in Kansas for further observation and testing. All tests reported them clean of the killing cells. Beta had not reappeared since Dr. Hamilton's questioning after Mr. Moore's recovery.

After several days of ridding stage four patients of cancer, the delegates, and Dell, met in a conference room on the shuttle pyramid to discuss their findings.

"Gentlemen, it is time for us to report our findings to our superiors," Dr. T'doyo said in her soothing sing-song voice. "What do we know? Please keep in mind, as Dr. Nelson pointed out, that this room may not be secure."

"Well, we have no more insights as to *why* and *how* our friends are helping us than we did when started," Dr. Nelson said.

"I know I am not an official delegate," said Dell, "but I can tell you that whatever this mystery process is, it works. We somehow cured over a dozen people of cancer. People who wouldn't have seen their grandkids, or run in the sun, or hugged their loved ones a year from now, could be alive long after we're gone. As far as I'm concerned, that makes it worth whatever they're after."

"Dr. Hamilton, do you believe they are being truthful with us?" Dr. T'doyo asked.

Everyone turned to Jeremy.

"I need to speak with Beta before I can give my final decision."

As soon as he said it, Jeremy Hamilton blinked out of existence.

*

"How can I help you, Dr. Hamilton?" Beta asked.

"I think after a few days of us eradicating cancer together, you can call me Jeremy." Hamilton looked around the crystal room he had just appeared in. Beta had faded into view just after he materialized.

"Very well ... Jeremy," Beta said hesitantly, "how can I help you?"

"You can start by telling me the truth."

"Why do you believe we are not being truthful with you?" the alien woman asked.

"You've been lying to us since you sent that drone to the White House lawn," Jeremy growled. "For starters, what do you really look like? You expect us to trust you and believe the story that you are just here to help us, but you aren't showing us your true form."

"Why would you say that?"

"Oh please. The bodies we first see are perfect in every way and almost *designed* to be specifically attractive to each of us and distracting from our mission. You bug our conference room, then 'overhear' us talk about your physical perfection and the next time we see you, just an hour later, you have subtle imperfections to make us feel more at ease with you." Jeremy points to his own feet. "You don't cast shadows and you never touch anything, including us. The problem with a seduction technique is that eventually you have to touch someone. You appeared so sexual, I was acutely aware of not ever touching you, even casually. When I '*accidentally*' pointed the hand scanner at you, nothing appeared on the screen. Not even a ghost of an image. And finally, you don't blink in and out the way your matter transfer device does to us. You 'come into focus' when you appear. If I had to guess, I would say you are holographic projections of some sort. Tell me I'm wrong."

Beta faded from sight.

"Beta? Hello? Anybody?" Jeremy bellowed at the white walls of the room.

All three aliens came into focus as he turned around the room. All three had their hands clasped behind their backs in their usual white frocks.

"Dr. Hamilton, Beta has relayed your concerns and we wish to—" Alpha began.

"Put a sock in it, E.T.," Jeremy punched his fist into the alien's chest.

Alpha looked down at the arm protruding from his sternum with no shock, pain, or surprise. Jeremy's face, on the other hand, was ashen white.

"Well, that could have gone horribly wrong," withdrawing his hand from the alien's torso.

"Now that you have surmised the nature of our interface, how can we help you Dr. Hamilton? We *are* here to help," Alpha said.

"You can start by answering some questions," Jeremy said, looking at his own hand which seconds before he had buried in the chest of the alien in front of him.

"Are you sure you really want the truth, Dr. Hamilton?" Delta asked flatly.

"That's all I've ever wanted my whole life," looking at each of the aliens one at a time. "The truth has hampered my career, ruined my marriage, and now, is very likely going to stop humanity from beating its worst enemy. Despite all that, damn straight I want the truth."

"Which truth would you like to start with?" Alpha asked. Jeremy noticed that Beta was strangely silent. "There are many truths. Some more personal than others."

"For starters, where do the cancer cells go?" Jeremy asked. "We transfer in saline, or that protein gel, and we 'beam' out the cancer. Where does it go? What do you do with it?"

Beta spoke for the first time since reappearing, "It's simple ... Jeremy. We eat it."

"YOU WHAT?" Jeremy exclaimed.

"We, our species that is, digest the cancer cells to live," Alpha explained. "We transfer them to storage units inside our main ship, and when we harvest all the carcinogenic material on your planet, we return to our home world to supply our populace with sustenance."

"You *eat* cancer?"

"Much the same way your planet's population survives on vegetables you grow on your farms," Delta explained. "There is no plot to subjugate your world. We have no interest in being responsible for feeding or controlling another planet."

Jeremy collapsed to a sitting position on the floor. This was almost more than he could handle. He thought he was prepared for the holographic deception, but the reality of what these creatures did with the cancer cells was too ... *alien* ... to ... *digest*. Several minutes passed while Jeremy processed what the alien images had told him.

"Wait. You said 'harvested' and 'grow on a farm.' Did you plant the seeds of cancer in us?"

"Galactic mandate forbids the manipulation of the genetic structure of other races to their detriment," Alpha stated.

"But ...?"

"Given the severity of our home world's dire situation, we did find a way to adhere to that mandate and still enable our civilization to survive," Delta said.

"So, you didn't break this galactic law, you just bent the hell out of it," Jeremy accused the aliens.

"No. We did not violate the rules set down," Alpha explained. "We did however, visit your world and adjust certain non-biological elements to better fertilize your environment. Unfortunately, one of our shuttles crashed in your North American desert only to be discovered. We have since made our presence less obtrusive."

"Desert? This wasn't about seventy-eighty years ago or so, was it?" Jeremy inquired.

"By your method of calculation, yes."

"Hold the phone. You 'adjusted certain non-biological elements to better fertilize our environment'?" Jeremy quoted.

"You speak a truth," stated Delta.

"So you didn't tamper with our DNA, but you monkeyed with our world ... so we would more easily get cancer?" Jeremy asked incredulously, looking directly at Beta.

"I am not certain of your vernacular, but I believe that to also be a truth," Delta explained.

"You didn't put cancer in us, not because it was wrong or anything, but it was against some cosmic law that you didn't want to get busted for. Then you made nearly everything else in our world cancerous? Because you were hungry," Jeremy exclaimed.

"We were *very* hungry."

"Dr. Hamilton, you must understand. We have waited for millennia as you quantify time to harvest these cells. It has taken this long for your populace's biologics to reach critical mass. We do this for the survival of our species," Alpha explained, as if to a petulant child.

"Do you know how many people have died from cancer while you waited for our world to 'ripen'?" Jeremy was nearly in tears. "My parents died because of what you did, waiting for your next meal, all the while you had the means to save them."

"We regret the inconvenience this may have caused you and anyone on your world," Alpha said, "but rest assured that once your governments accept our offer, that no one on Earth will suffer from cancer for several generations."

"Several generations?" Jeremy asked.

"Yes. The environmental and elemental conditions still exist on your world," Delta explained. "We will remove all cancer cells currently in any humans, but eventually, the environment will create carcinomas in new generations to come."

"But why?" Jeremy asked. "Why not just eliminate all those cancer-causing agents in our world?"

"Why does one of your farmers not burn his fields after a single harvest? He wants to harvest again next season."

"Next—" Jeremy was aghast. "You mean you're going to let cancer start growing in us again?"

"Yes," Delta said. "It will take several of your generations before it reaches a critical mass that justifies sending a craft back to harvest again. Surely you must realize this is not the only world we are 'farming.'"

"But you said our governments have a choice."

"We are not conquerors. We do not dictate the actions of others," Alpha said. "Your world has the choice to allow us to harvest these cells and be on our way, or forever allow cancer to decimate your population."

"That's no choice!" bellowed Jeremy. "What world would let so many suffer and die when there is a free solution?"

"Actually, Jeremy," Beta said quietly. "Your world's governing bodies await your verdict on whether we have their best interests at heart. They do not choose. You do."

"You expect me to decide if a large chunk of population lives or dies horribly? That's unfair!"

"More so than you think, Dr. Hamilton," Alpha stated.

"What could be more awful than that?" Jeremy asked of the alien.

"The scanner we loaned you for testing, transmitted data back to us as you used it. When you used it on yourself. We know."

*

Jeremy Hamilton appeared back at the F.O.B. soon after. Dell quickly hustled him into an empty Quonset hut.

"Doc, where have you been? What's going on?"

"Dell, there's some things I want you to do for me," Jeremy began. "I want you to write up all our notes into a paper—hell! several papers—and submit them to every medical and scientific journal in the world."

127

"But Doc," Dell said "they'll end up giving whoever writes those papers all the credit. He'll get the Nobel prize in medicine. He'll be on the cover of every magazine in the world as the man who brought the cure to cancer to Earth. It should be you who writes them. I'm glad to help, but you were the point man on this thing."

"No, I need you to promise me you will do this. Also, I want another promise from you. A serious one."

"More serious than taking all the credit for curing cancer? Sure, Doc, no problem."

"I want you to swear to me that you will continue to search for a real cure, or reverse engineer the alien transfer technology, so that we are not dependent on them to save us. Can you do that?" Hamilton gripped his assistant by both shoulders. "At the very least, inspire others to continue the work. There are things in the environment that are causing these cancers. Find them."

"Yeah, but why?" Dell asked. "In a few weeks, won't Carmen Elektra and her pals eliminate the need for oncologists, period?"

"Promise me."

"Sure, Doc. After all, you're forcing me to be the hero of the medical and scientific world, the least I can do is swear my life's work to a field that won't exist soon."

*

"And that, ladies and gentlemen, is my report," Jeremy Hamilton concluded to the E.I.O. committee.

"And that's it?" the senior intelligence officer asked. "You are telling us to trust the aliens and that this 'cure' they're offering seems legitimate and that they have no ulterior motives?"

Jeremy looked at the other two delegates seated to his side.

"Unless you have evidence to the contrary, yes, that is what I am saying."

"Well, Ah guess that's it then," the chairman announced. "Our experts are of the opinion that it is jest about impossible for you to lie about something so important Dr. Hamilton. We will let the alien shuttle crafts start removing cancer from patients in every major city. Free of charge. This will decimate the pharmaceutical industry." *Companies that have major interests and investments in my constituency.*

"There is just one other thing gentlemen," Jeremy interjected. "My assistant, Dell, will be publishing extensively on the data we collected and I expect your full support for him on this."

"Why aren't *you* publishing, Doctor?" the chairman asked.

"Because I am going with our new friends. First to their main ship and then back with them to their home planet once they have eradicated cancer from Earth."

The room silenced.

"Is it the woman, Beta?" the intelligence officer asked.

"No. She is not someone I can envision myself holding," Jeremy said. "I am going because there are more truths out in the galaxy and I wish to live long enough to discover them. I hope someday to be able to provide Earth with some of them. I also believe there are some galactic law makers that would love to talk to me."

*

Two days later, Dr. Jeremy Hamilton found himself lying on a bed in the alien craft.

Beta, or at least her image, stood beside him.

"You are sure this something you wish to do, Jeremy?" Beta asked.

"Yes. If you keep your promise to me."

"I will," Beta replied.

Moments later, the alien machines finished their work and Dr. Jeffrey Hamilton's body showed no signs of pancreatic cancer. Beta had promised him that she, in her real body, would be the one to digest his cancer cells. As of right now, he was cancer-free.

***

Follicles, Fables & Follies
Rapunzel, Rapunzel, let down ... never mind

Once upon a time (because that's how all the really good stories start) a king and a queen lived in a beautiful castle (only very rarely do you ever hear of a king and queen living in an *ugly* castle). They had everything they ever wanted. Almost. They longed a child for years but were never able to reproduce. At long last, and after nearly a decade of serious effort, the queen relayed to the king that they are expecting. The crown invited royalty and aristocracy from all the known world to a magnificent celebration.

During these revelries, stories drifted to the king and queen of a faraway land where gorgeous fields of a delicate, purple, bell-shaped flower called rampion, the roots of which can be eaten in salads and are said to be quite delicious grew. (Pretty much irrelevant to the main gist of our story, but damned few folks these days know about rampion.) More relevant to the story is that these fields, among others, were owned and protected by an old crone of a witch, who guarded her possessions rabidly. Despite that, the more the queen thought about these beautiful plants, the more she obsessed over them.

"If I can't eat some of that mythical root, I shall surely die," she whined to the king.

Her preoccupation grew until he could not bear to see his wife do without the roots a moment longer.

The monarch made a proclamation to his kingdom. "It matters not whether it is the cravings of a mother-to-be, or the desires of my queen, I shall travel to this faraway land and procure this delicacy for my own royal flower."

The king and his royal guards (you didn't think he was going alone, did you?) set out and travelled to the faraway land. They journeyed long, crossing sea and land to a southern continent. After they disembarked and unloaded their steeds and accoutrement (that's French for "stuff"), it took them weeks of hunting and following clues to find the witch's fields. Once they arrived and encountered no witch, the king set his guards to collect the plants.

"Your majesty," the head of his royal guard reported, bowed low before his king. The king sat impatiently upon his tent's temporary throne. "The flowers of these plants are white and not the beautiful purple we were told."

The king thought long and hard on this. "Perhaps they are out of season. Maybe the stories were from when they bloom."

"Your highness, they grow in clusters on shrubs or on vines, not in waving fields of flowers."

"The stories during the celebration didn't have all the details," the king replied.

"But your excellency," the guard warned, "the stems of these plants exude a milky substance that burns your guards' hands on contact."

"Must I do all your thinking for you?" the king growled. "Then. Don't. Touch. The stems. Only collect the roots."

During the sea voyage north, the monarch looked out over the waves and gestured to his guard. "That went rather well, I would think. Rumors say that the roots are the delicious part and I doubt the flowers, white or purple, would have survived the trek home."

The master of guards looked down on his blistered hand resting atop the satchel of roots and said, "Yes, sire. Her majesty will no doubt be quite satisfied."

*

"I WANT MORE!" the queen screeched at the top of her lungs.

"But dear, as soon as we returned," the king replied, "I gave a sample of the roots to the royal sage and that was only a day or so ago. He is looking through his ancient tomes to make sure they are safe for you to eat."

"I couldn't wait for that old fool," the queen glared. "I had those roots made into a salad and they were so delicious, I devoured them already. I must have more. Much more. It's bad enough that it took you ages to get back here with them. Look at me. I am growing like a cow with your child."

"But my beloved, the voyage was perilous and long. We risked the wrath of the evil witch that hordes her precious flowers. Surely what we brought back satisfied your cravings."

"GET. ME. MORE." With one hand cradling her slightest of baby bumps, she stormed from the room.

*

"My loyal subjects," the announcement began. "We have decided that we have not provided our dear queen with as much of the rare root as she requires for the safe and healthy future bearing of our royal heir. I will once more venture into the southern realms and procure this delicacy. Now that we know the exact location of the fields, we should be back in your presence in a fraction of the time. My queen shall have what she desires no matter what the cost."

*

"Your majesty," the royal sage bowed as he entered the queen's chambers. "Has his majesty set off on his quest yet?"

"Just this morning, no thanks to you," her highness said, as she admired herself in a mirror. "What do you need, you old curmudgeon?"

Cradling an archaic text in one hand and brushing his wisp of a white beard with the other, the ancient advisor chortled, "Oh. Nothing. Nothing that can't wait until he returns."

*

As the king and his men approached the fields in the southern continent where they first procured the roots, a hoary crone greeted them.

"Why do you come to my fields, your magnificence?" the crone asked, eyeing their regal clothing and mounts.

"My queen yearns for the root of these plants, and have them she shall," the monarch stated.

"You dare to enter my realm," her eyes flaring red light as a wind sprang forth to whip their hair and clothing, "descend into my garden and steal my property like a thief in the night?"

The king, noting the change in the crone's demeanor and sensing her power, changed his tone.

"My dear woman, I come before you not as a monarch to a mighty kingdom, but as a husband trying to alleviate the suffering of his wife with child. She has tasted a small portion of these plants and must have more or die."

The witch pondered his words. "If it is as you say, you may take as much of these plants as you and your men can carry ... on one condition."

"And what is that, fair woman?" the king asked, forgetting the needs of his wife entirely, terrified for his own life.

"You must give me your soon-to-be newborn child," the hag cackled. "I will feed it and care for it like a mother."

The king, now near incontinent with fright, bowed his head and whispered, "It shall be as you ask."

*

The king returned with all the roots the queen could have made into salads for months. After a few days, the queen tired of salads and now craved something else. Time passed. With the exception of her majesty's pregnancy, life was as it always was in the castle. After a time, the king forgot his vow to the witch.

Finally, the big day arrived and the royal hand maidens helped deliver the most beautiful little girl-child in the land.

The king paced nervously outside her chambers while his sage leaned heavily on a gnarled walking stick. Upon hearing the cry of the newborn, the king burst into the room just as the witch appeared in an eruption of smoke and flame, snatched the child from the mother, and winked conspiratorially at the king.

"WHAT HAVE YOU DONE?" the queen screeched at her husband from the bed.

Before the horrified monarch could answer his wife, the hag announced, "I shall name her Rapunzel." And disappeared with the child in an outpouring of flame and smoke.

"Rapunzel?" the sage rubbed his beard, thinking back. "That was the name of the plant you brought her majesty to eat. It wasn't rampion, it was rapunzel."

*

Years rolled by. The king and queen never did have another child, primarily due to the fact that the queen never forgave the king or let him touch her again.

Stories of a strange, young, blonde girl-child wandering in a faraway land occasionally travelled to the court. After a tale of how this beautiful child wandered into the home of a family of bears, the stories mysteriously dried up. The royal couple feared that this could be their lost child and that she was eaten by the bears. The king became even more isolated, withdrawn, and distant, while the queen vented her ire at all around her.

The castle finally became ugly.

*

"Have I not treated you like my own?" the witch barked at Rapunzel.

"Yes, mum," the child answered dutifully.

"Have I not given you the freedom to wander my land and learn what you will? Do you lack for anything?"

"Just other people, mum."

"Don't get me started about all that trouble with the little miners. Your beauty and golden locks may have fooled them, but I am impervious to your guile. Well, loneliness is no reason to wander into the midst of a sloth of bears, sleep in their home, and eat their food," the enchantress said. "I think from now on, I need to confine you to keep out of trouble."

With a wave of her hand, the witch created a colossal tower with gleaming walls of smooth jewel and neither stairs nor doors. At the very top was a large window. In an explosion of smoke and flame, she transported Rapunzel and herself to the room at the top. To one side of the grand room was a small fountain of clear water and on the other side of the room a small privy that fed into the tower below.

"Are you all right, mum?" Rapunzel asked the witch, seeing her benefactor lean on the bedpost.

"I'm fine. That just took a lot more out of me than it used to. Give me a few moments to recover."

"What is this place?" asked the child.

"This, my dear, is where you spend the rest of your life," the hag stated. "No more wandering, no more trouble, no more people, no more incidents. I will bring you food and your playthings, but your days of causing grief are over."

"No mum! Please don't! I'll be good. I won't be bad anymore. I promise."

"I'm sorry, child, but it's in everyone's best interest that you remain here forever."

*

As time passed, the witch's powers waned. She denied it, even to herself, but the truth of the matter was: it became nearly impossible to teleport and completely futile to attempt to conjure objects from thin air. The gleaming tower was the last thing she had manifested and it sapped nearly all of her power. It took the last dregs of her sorcery to maintain her inhuman physical strength.

Even though she loathed to admit it, the witch's powers continued to fade. She foresaw this day approaching and refused to let Rapunzel cut her long, blonde hair, all the while teaching her to braid it.

At first, the witch brought Rapunzel fresh food and fruit every day. But as the years passed and her abilities weakened, she was no longer able to teleport and the deliveries became more infrequent. Sometimes she would come every week and some as little as every month. By that time, much of the food was dead, rotten, or spoiled.

No longer able to transport to the tower's room, she would strap the food to her back, stand at the tower's base, and call out:

"Rapunzel, Rapunzel, let down your hair, so that I may climb thy golden stair!"

A long, thick braid of blonde hair would unfurl from the tower's window and the witch would climb it to the top.

*

"What would you have me do, my dear?" the king implored of his angry queen.

"You're the king. Think of something. Must I do all your thinking for you?"

"We sent knights and guards to the area where we found the roots—"

"The *rapunzel* roots!" the queen snapped.

"The rapunzel roots. But no sign of our daughter or the witch was found. We sent messengers to every kingdom to learn of any word, and in all this time, all we have heard back are some rumors of a crystal tower," the king replied.

"Well, she was kidnapped years ago and who knows what horrors she has suffered at the hands of that hag. I want her back NOW. We are not getting any younger, you know."

"No," the king sighed, "we are not."

"I know what I will do," exclaimed the king. "I will put out a challenge. Anyone who rescues our daughter may have her hand in marriage! Surely that will get some results."

"You will do no such thing. What if some commoner saves her? Then we have some peasant as a son-in-law," the queen snarled.

"Wouldn't it be better to have our daughter back safe and sound and married to a commoner than tortured at the hands of a witch?"

"No."

"What if I were to allow only princes or royal blood to enter the challenge?" the king asked his wife. "That way, we get our daughter back and strengthen our kingdom."

"Well, as long as he's from a *rich* kingdom."

*

"Twenty-two princes we have sent out and twenty-two times each has failed to return," the queen stated accusingly.

"I know. The other kingdoms are reluctant to send any more princes. We seem to lose them," the king replied. "There is one more waiting in the foyer now. I have a good feeling about this one. Twenty-third time is a charm. Twenty-three has always been my lucky number."

"Not mine. That was the age you were when we got married," the queen responded.

*

"My boy, all the resources of the kingdom will be at your disposal in an effort to rescue our daughter," the king announced to the latest prince to accept the challenge. "We have the clues deduced by our sages. We have the rumors from all the kingdoms of where this crystal tower may be. Our royal coffers are open to you to fund your journey. We will provide you with the finest mounts, armor, and weaponry. Our mages will provide you with talismans and amulets to protect you from the witchcraft of the sorceress. Anything you need, you have but to ask."

"Thank you, your divine majesties. I will do all in my power to return your lovely daughter to her palatial home," the young prince said. "It is said that at birth, she was the fairest beauty in any kingdom."

"She was tolerable," the aging queen whispered.

"With your permissions, I will take my leave and begin my quest in the morn," the prince stated, bowing as he exited the royal chamber.

"He seems like a nice lad," the king said. "Good looking, smart, heroic. A good catch for our daughter when he brings her back."

"Well," the queen replied, "she won't lack for having her ass kissed."

*

The prince (we'll call him "Bob"), finally found the crystal tower. It was not far from the land where the king and his men found the rapunzel roots, but the spell that had kept it hidden had long faded. Prince Bob camped in the woods near the tower (there's always a nearby woods) and watched for the witch and any movement in the tower window. After a few days, he saw no sign of the sorceress and only the tiniest of movement in the window at the top of the tower. He stealthily made his way to the tower looking for an entrance. He could find no door and the walls were too smooth to find any purchase to climb. He retreated to the woods to resume his vigil.

After a few days, the witch hobbled to the keep carrying a bag on her back. The bag seemed to move of its own accord. He watched in rapt fascination as she called out:

"Rapunzel, Rapunzel, let down your hair, so that I may climb thy golden stair!"

And just like that, Prince Bob had his way in.

Prince Bob watched for days and the witch never came back out. He decided that she must have descended while he was asleep. Surely, no one would willingly confine themselves to an unscalable tower. It would no doubt drive them mad.

*

Prince Bob made his way to the tower, pausing frequently to look for the return of the witch. At the base and after a final glance around, Prince Bob called up:

"Rapunzel, Rapunzel, let down your hair, so that I may climb thy golden stair!"

After several moments, a thick braided rope of golden hair unfurled from the window. To make it easier to climb, Bob removed his armor and ensured his magical talismans were secure. He reached up, grabbed the braid, and inserted his toes into the braids for the climb.

Partway up the tower, Prince Bob, with the excitement of his adventure giving way to the physical exhaustion of climbing, began to notice small things. The braid had an oily feel to it and a slightly unpleasant aroma.

Closer to the window, Prince Bob noticed that the braid had, at some point, changed from gold to silver. *How enchanted must the princess be that she has hair made of both gold and silver? She is worth a fortune and we are soon to be wed.*

Finally reaching the window, the exhausted prince fell over the ledge in a clatter and sat spent beneath the sill, looking about the room for his new bride.

*

The first thing Prince Bob noted was the size of the room. He hadn't realized that the tower was very broad and that it didn't narrow as it ascended. The room was gigantic and dark. In the gloom, he couldn't see the far—

WHAT IS THAT STENCH?

A wall of odor assaulted his senses like a hammer. The tower reeked of blood and bad meat. An abattoir of death and blood. Clamping his hand over his mouth and nose, he leaned to one side in preparation of spewing his meager breakfast. Still sitting on the floor, unable to gain his footing due to fatigue and the shock of revulsion, he wrapped his sash around his nose and mouth to help stave off the fetid smell of rot.

As his eyes adjusted to the dim lighting, provided by the gloom outside the window, he spied two enormous bear pelts, one on the floor and one on the wall. The fur on the wall was larger than the one on the floor, but both looked old and not prepared properly. They appeared scraped off the bear carcasses by hand without the use of any tools. No tannery made these rugs.

Staggering to his feet, Prince Bob stepped a few paces into the dark room. The room was awash in blood, both old and freshly tacky. His senses rebelled. What kind of horror had this witch subjected to his new fiancée?

It was then that an impact from the darkness knocked Bob completely unconscious.

*

Finding himself in a sitting position on the hard floor (again), Prince Bob awoke with blinding pain at the back of his head. Whether from being knocked unconscious or from the horrific stench, he promptly threw up all over the blood-soaked floor. Unable to catch himself with his hands, he hit the floor face first, inches from his own bile. Struggling, Prince Bob quickly discovered his hands were tied behind his back, his feet bound securely by ropey twine.

Knocked unconscious, painfully bound and captured, smeared with blood from the floor, weak from disgorging his breakfast, and physically drained from climbing the tower. This was NOT how he pictured his first big adventure.

Prince Bob stretched his neck to look around the room and perhaps see the harpy who had knocked him unconscious and tied him. Farthest from the window, he could not make out the details of the face, but could see eyes in the darkness and hear chewing, snarling, lip-smacking noises as she ate.

Bob backed away from the eyes staring at him from the darkness as much as he could, bound as he was. He could see the braid of hair he had climbed looped around a bed post, trailing into the recesses of the room.

"Ho, hateful witch. What have you done with my beloved Rapunzel?" Prince Bob bellowed toward the darkness. "As soon as I free myself, I shall end your evil crusade and you shall torture that poor girl no more!"

As he stared straight ahead into the darkness, Bob saw that the eyes never moved, never blinked. Only a deep growl came from the darkness in response.

From his right, hidden behind the massive bed, he heard a faint cough. Without looking away from the eyes glaring at him from the dark, Prince Bob inched toward the sound of the cough.

Bob nearly gagged again as he edged around the corner of the mattress and shifted his eyes momentarily to the bedside— where he saw the witch with both her legs amputated.

*

"What trickery is this?" Prince Bob demanded.

The witch barely opened her eyes as the corners of her bloodless lips curled into a smile. Her raw stumps of legs tourniqueted with the same ropy twine that bound Bob's feet and hands.

"No tricks, young fool. I am here as I have sat for days, kept alive only by my remaining magicks. Amazing what you can do when your back is literally against the wall."

"If you are here, then that is ...?" the prince stammered, glancing back into the gloom.

"Not what you expected, I'd wager."

"How did this come to be?"

"I hope I have the energy to both enlighten you and sustain my life. Given my condition and this situation, maybe eternal sleep would be a blessing. I suppose the telling will help pass the time.

"When she was a child," the witch began, "she would wander into the woods and get into no ends of trouble. She seduced and butchered a house full of dwarfish miners once. I never did find two of the bodies. In the middle of an incident with a family of grizzlies, I locked her in this tower. As my power dwindled with age, I was unable to find sustenance for her close by and had to travel farther and farther to hunt for her. I still had a smidgeon of my power left, so one at a time, I transported the three bears she tortured to her room as playthings to keep her occupied while I hunted. Evidently, she was hungrier than I thought. That's their skins you see on the walls and floor. The third one was just her size.

"My hunts to find her food took me away for most of the time. I found out later that during the months I hunted, twenty different princes found their way here just as you have. As I said, she was hungrier than I imagined. The twenty-first prince saw her from his perch on the window and leapt to his death. She coerced me into tying his broken body to her braids and she hauled his remains up to this room. The twenty-second, I deliberately let climb and enter as I watched, knowing his ultimate fate. By that time, I tired of constantly hunting.

"A few days ago, I returned with ... shall we say 'youthful' sustenance from a faraway village when she attacked me. Weak from the climb, I was an easy victim. After she devoured my offering, she grew hungry again, but realized that by keeping me alive, her food source will not rot as quickly if it is kept alive. Hence, the tourniquets. Her hunger has evidently overpowered her common sense, for without me to hunt for her, how does she expect to get new fare? I mean, other than idiots like yourself."

A shape emerged from the gloom. The fetid butcher's smell grew stronger as it approached. Thick braids of hair once golden, now fell gray from her scalp, trailed to the loops around the bedpost. Skin so white from lack of light that it was nearly transparent hanging from muscles and tendons. Fingernails, chipped and bloody, curled from the end of her claw-like hands. The mouth exuded a foul stench from between rotten and blackened teeth. Perhaps most foul was the scraped fur of a young bear cub, with putrid meat still clinging to its pelt, draped over the shoulders of this apparition.

"Now that I have enough to eat for the time being, you and I have time to get to know each other better," the ghoulish figure croaked as it stepped closer to him. "The others said that my father promised them my hand in marriage if they found me. Well, you found me. You begged to climb up my tresses. Do you want to know a secret? I have never been with a man before. You can be my first."

Eyes wide with terror, Prince Bob scrambled back toward the window as best he could, tied hand and foot.

"Witch!" he screamed. "You did this. You locked her away, starved her, tortured her, turned her into this creature, all to protect her from what you think of as a cruel world."

"You sad, sad fool!" the witch hissed. "The rapunzel root the king fed his wife all those years ago poisoned the unborn infant's mind. It's true I locked Rapunzel in this tower for the rest of her life. Not to protect her from the world, but to protect the world FROM HER."

And Rapunzel lived happily ever after ... for a while.

***

A New York Yankee
Time traveling baseball player upends King Arthur's court

I remember everything. Right up until the gigantic cracker
cold-cocked me. Oh, I remember a bunch of stuff after I wake
up, but that has to be a dream, right?

My boys and I are doing what all professional ballplayers
do just before the World Series: Partying.

The limo, an enormous, vintage, petrol-burner, dropped us
off outside whatever "in" club in Manhattan reigns these days
at one a.m. Artie told the driver to wait for us, "we'd be an
hour or so." Artie adores the idea of giving orders to white
guys. It may be 2056, but racial lines are drawn sharply enough
you could cut yourself. White people are so afraid of offending
us; they treat us like royalty. It's good to be the king.

Artie and L compete to talk trash to the same waiter,
confident in the fact one of them will take him home.
Whatever. Takes all kinds. While race issues became more
volatile in recent years, sexual orientation has become a non-
issue. Artie and L leapt out of the closet when they were kids,
and as the two best outfielders in the league, no one cares.
Care? Some feel it makes our team that much cooler.

I surpass my physical limits of alcohol consumption and am rounding third on a hookup with a red-headed, young hottie sitting at the bar, wearing about half a dress. She was wearing the dress. Not me. My motto is: "*What Mrs. Patricia Morgan, and the MLB, don't know, won't hurt me.*" (One will slap my hand with a fine, and one will make me dance on the end of a butcher knife. I'll let you guess who will do what.) I slide my iPal out of my inner jacket pocket to pay the bill. Evidently, *we* bought the house a couple of rounds. Makes me think of money. I pause to send an encrypted vmail to Rudy. As I swipe to send, a shadow eclipses the lights from the dance floor.

The eclipse turns out to be the most massive white man I've ever seen. By far. And I play professional sports. Godzilla screams at me, red veins popping out on his non-existent neck. All I can hear is part of the word "girlfriend" over the music as he hauls a ham-sized fist back to bludgeon me. The world moves in slow motion. Artie and L will never make it in time. I slide the iPal back into my jacket to cover reaching for my nine out of my back waistband. A million thoughts race through my head at once. I hesitate. If I pop this giant, my multi-gazillion dollar contract disappears, and ... oh yeah ... my baseball career. On the other hand, if he removes my head from my shoulders, which looks to be a solid bet, that would likely end it too. We could fight, and even as mountainous as I am for a ballplayer, Godzilla is much BIGGER. I have as much chance against this guy as Artie and L have of going straight. The press won't see it that way. The commissioner won't see it that way. I'll end up sued. Again. Turns out, I have no choice in the matter.

The last thing I see before all the lights fade: a tarnished high school ring. Real, real close.

*

CRASH LANDING

Damn! Someone used my head for batting practice. I push my way into what might be loosely described as an upright sitting position against a tree, just as some yahoo rides up on a horse. An honest-to-God horse! You see them in zoos, but even mounted cops are motorized these days.

I stand up to see who can afford to own a horse, much less ride one. And there it is. A guy in a suit of medieval armor. Museum quality. Makes perfect sense. Brain damage. Godzilla scrambled my eggs pretty thoroughly.

"Who be your master, boy?" he demands. English accent. Snotty as all hell.

"Watch that 'boy' shit, cracker." I try to be as race neutral as I can be, but Armor-All has crossed all kinds of lines.

"Impudence! If you be a free-roaming Moor, then I claim you for House Gwalchmei." He pulls out an extremely long sword and points it at me, still sitting in the saddle. I search around for the camera; sure my boys are screwing with me.

Or maybe not. He presses the point into my jacket lapel.

I can still sense the nine in the waistband of my jeans (Thank God!), but I don't consider Mr. Hallucination here as *that* much of a threat. Plus, if this *is* a practical joke, it might suck all the fun out of it if I cap this racist tin can here and now.

I step back a pace or two, pick up a hefty fallen tree branch, tap it on the bottom of my shoe, and line drive his ass right off the back of the horse. His dismount looks painful and sounds worse.

I stand over Armor-All, teeing-up on his bucket head.

"I ... yield," he stammers. "State your terms, Moor."

"The name's Morgan. Not Moor. Henry Morgan." I pick up his sword. It's much heavier than I imagined. I take a long dagger from his belt. I don't see a gun on him. "Stand up. You look stupid laying there."

"I require ... assistance."

*

WHAT'S IN A NAME?

It takes both of us to haul him off the ground. His suit of armor weighs a ton. I help him take his helmet off. Whoa.

Long, brown, greasy hair; dirty, unkempt beard; and smells as if he hasn't bathed in weeks. Except for being short and white, he could be a professional basketball player.

"Did you state that your name be ... Morgan? By chance, be you related to Morguause, of the House Lot?" the knight asks.

"Not that I know of. Born and bred in the city so nice, they had to name it twice. 'Hammerin' Hank Morgan, starting catcher for the New York Yankees. You probably saw me on TV. Sorry, man, I can't do autographs. I licensed my signature to Hallmark last season."

Armor-All doesn't know what to do with that. Clearly not a sports fan. Bitch.

"Do you know who my mother is?" Armor-All asks.

"No. Do you?" I'm still a little heated over the whole "master" and "boy" thing.

"I ask of your relationship to Morguause, as I am her son, Gwalchmei, loyal nephew and knight to our liege, the King. My aunt's name be Morgen. If related to her, it begs to ask in regards to your ... lineage." Old Gwalchmei knows how to sugar coat the fact auntie dearest may have been doing little "slumming." Well, she wouldn't be the first white sister looking for the LD, won't be the last.

Gwalchmei shakes his greasy head. "'Tis no matter. You bested me, albeit in a somewhat unorthodox manner. How say you, Henry of the House Morgan? What be your terms?"

"G-man, I just want to catch a ride back home and make the Series."

"Even bested as I am, I cannot offer a Moor to ride while I walk alongside as a knave, but I can walk beside thee."

Give him credit. He's offering me the back of the bus, but at least he's back there with me.

"I know not where your home is. Truthfully, I understand little of your strange speech. But I can offer you hearth, home, suitable attire, and sustenance. Perhaps an audience with Our Majesties."

"Lead on, McDuff."

"No. It's Gwalchmei."

*

YAY FOR CHINESE MANUFACTURING!

As we walk, I slide my iPal out of my jacket. It's undamaged, thankfully. One improvement over the years involved toughening these things up. You could hit one with a hammer and not ding it. Unfortunately, Godzilla hit a whole lot harder than a hammer. They measure battery life in months now, not days.

No chips, cracks, or dents. Or signal. How is that even possible? Decades ago, the entire country went WI-FI3. Years before, wireless networking blanketed the globe. It should be impossible not to detect something. I check the latest download date. Last night. Just before we hit the town (no pun intended). At least this thing has most of the Internet downloaded to it.

"Pal, why am I not getting a signal?" I ask the screen.

"I don't understand, my dark friend," Gwalchmei says believing I am talking to him.

"*I can theorize we are not in the United States as the Internet Accessibility Act of 2032 provided for free, unlimited access to the Internet and mobile communications to all within its borders, with certain restrictions applying.*" Okay, maybe calling my iPal's female-voiced assistant software "Pal" strikes even me as a little weird.

"WITCHCRAFT!" Gwalchmei screams. Stepping back as fast as his steel plate will allow, he looks around for a woman.

"Relax, G. It's just my iPal. Surely, they're all over ... Hey! Where are we?"

Gwalchmei never takes his gaze off my iPal, eyeing it with suspicion and fear. "We be but a few leagues from my home inside the castle of Lord of all the Britains."

"Great Britain? Maybe they don't maintain universal access here." Not beyond Artie and L to ship my unconscious ass to England as a practical joke. I can't see them doing it just before the Series, but as I mentioned, there was more than a little alcohol involved.

"Pal, call Coach." He will fly me back to the States and the playoffs on the fastest thing moving. If he doesn't fire me.

"*I am unable to detect or connect to any mobile communication or WI-FI networks at this time. Please try your call later.*"

"I do not understand, Friend Henry, but the wizened Myrddin will fathom this sorcerous peril."

"Smartest guy at the Renaissance Festival, huh? Fine." Rolling with it. "Pal, is this England?"

"*I am unable to connect to any GPS signals at this time. Please try again later.*"

Damn. GPS is *global* positioning. Maybe I did break the friggin' thing.

*

OKAY, NOT THE RENAISSANCE FESTIVAL

These guys must be some sort of re-enactment freaks, dressing up in Days of Yore. Still doesn't answer how they got here. No parking lot. In my few days here, not one person breaks character or uses an iPal, or any modern convenience I can see. No running water. No refrigerator. No microwave. Not even chewing gum. These guys are good. Too good.

And then there's the smell. Shit. I mean real shit. I see people throwing sewage out into the street. The smell of animals and manure hangs far and wide, and that's just marginally worse than the people. Gwalchmei's home boasts an outdoor "privy," essentially, a semi-enclosed hole in the ground. Go ahead. Ask me about toilet paper. "Personal hygiene," two words these people can't even spell. One thing worse than their body odor is their breath. When you get close (and don't!), check out some of these people's teeth, you'll see why. I used to fancy Gwalchmei as ripe. After meeting some castle dwellers, my boy G's all but surgically sterile.

If it's a re-enactment group, they're dedicated to the point of bag-of-hammers crazy. The food's so disgusting, you won't see it on a reality show and the drinking water is not quite brown, but it's well on its way. I settle for some undercooked meat and wine.

*

MIDDLE AGES

I learn something a few nights later I wish I hadn't.

"Friend Henry, how old be you? I hold no experience with Moors, so I bear no way to gauge your age," Gwalchmei asks during some confusing, but polite, conversation.

"I am not a—never mind. Well, G, you've hit a bit of a sore point with ball players. I'm coming up on thirty-six, which is up there in Major League years."

"Ah. Beyond middle-aged. 'Tis disheartening facing our twilight years, but t'is God's will."

"Whoa! Hold on there, Armor All. Thirty-six ain't old. My whole life's ahead of me. I could squeak out a few more years of ball if I take care of myself." I am more than a little pissed. Racial slurs I can swallow, but trash talking a ball player's age and it's game on. I size Gwalchmei up and down, figuring him in his late-fifties. "Uh, how old are you, G?"

"I meant no offense, Friend Henry. I am in no position to cast aspersions on your vigor. My mother bore me mid-month of May, in 492 Anno Domini. So I am unquestionably old as well. I am approaching my thirty-second winter."

"Thirty-second! G, no apologies necessary for me, but I thought you are a LOT older than—WAIT! Did you say '492 Anno Domini'? As in 'AD?'" I do some quick math, never strong suit for me. I sit for a moment, taking it in. "Is this 523 AD?"

"Aye, my dark friend. I know, more than ever, Their Majesties will wish to meet an enchanted Moor of advanced years, who appears so youthful, *and* can cipher. In truth, it be beyond imagining."

No. Shit.

*

"Friend Henry, I secured an audience with Their Majesties a fortnight from now. I did not presume it possible to procure an audience so soon, but it seems Her Highness has never seen an ensorcelled Moor before," Gwalchmei announces.

"A fortnight? What's that? A couple of days from now?"

"No, my tall friend. A fortnight be fourteen days."

"G! I need to shag my butt back to the States *right now*. The World Series starts soon, and if I am not at practice, I can kiss my sweet, sweet contract goodbye."

"I'm sorry, Friend Henry, but Their Majesties cannot see you until then, and the sole chance you to return you home involves a mounted escort and letters of conduct from them."

"They'll want me to mount an escort?" I ask incredulously. Clearly, the bar hottie did not work out as planned. I avoided "Trish Da Bitch" for longer than our usual few weeks and mounting an escort sounds pretty tasty right about now.

"If your audience goes well, His Majesty may grant you a boon to ride all the way," Gwalchmei says.

"Okay. I'm up for it if she is." Somehow, I don't think we're talking the same thing.

*

I AM SO SCREWED

I've decided to not fixate on what I can't figure and focus on the few facts in my possession.

I seem to be in Great Britain. At any rate, the lot of them speak with a barely understandable British accent.

My iPal can't find a GPS, mobile, or WI-FI network. But it works. Just no connectivity. Just no way to communicate with anyone. Great.

I am in a castle. Out in the sticks with nothing around for miles and miles.

I am not going to make it back for the Series. Thank God I got a vmail off to Rudy.

I still carry my Ruger, though I gave Gwalchmei back his sword and knife. I wouldn't know how to use them anyway, and he didn't stab me as soon as he got them, so I have that going for me. Pretty sure I'm safe since he put me up in his home and feeds me, be that as it may.

Until I see proof to the contrary, I am going to accept (and it pains me to even consider this) I am stuck ... in the sixth century.

Oh yeah, I'm the sole brother in the castle.

*

MY KINGDOM FOR CHEESEBURGER!

I thought I could take it, but I can't.

"G, I need to eat some real food, a bath, and some clean clothes."

"Dost thou imagine the food be fictional, Friend Henry?" Gwalchmei thinks I'm simple *and* possessed.

"No, I appreciate what you've done for me. At least, let me help out around here. I have some ideas to make this place much cooler," I try a different tack.

"Art thou *hot?*" Gwalchmei a lot of things, but speedy on the uptake is not one of them.

"No, G, I mean with a little work, we can hook you up with the most bitchin' house in the whole castle."

"Why would I wish to tether my house to dogs, Friend Henry?"

"Never mind. Just tell your servants to do what I instruct them to do. Trust me."

"It shall be as you will, my dark friend. And I do trust you. You defeated me soundly and gave me back my blade. You speak true, though strangely. No man could ask for more."

I can.

*

Clean water. It all depends on clean water. G has servants take care of his household, and while they do all that I ask, they do it when not doing their usual chores for Gwalchmei. Can't blame them for knowing the relationship of their bread and buttered, I guess. I coerce G's maids into boiling well water on a regular basis to purify it. Boiled water supplements what we fetch from a nearby stream ... from upstream. You do not want to know how the water smells downstream. While collecting water, I take time to bathe and wash my clothes. I notice Gwalchmei's maids peeking and giggling. They've never seen a brother before. Well, once you go twenty-first century, you never go back.

*

Now we can drink safely, wash our clothes, cook and clean. I convince G's staff to bathe at least a couple of times a week, but many suspect this is how the Devil enters. After many arguments, I convince the women through their sense of smell. First, I had to convince them *why* they should smell better. I can't find it in myself to launch into a lecture on microscopic germs, viruses, and bacteria, so I do what Mamma used to, and say, "Because I said so." And now I know why she said it: it works.

The men are easier. The household women would withhold their "favors" until the men did not smell pig-like. Same rules apply to using a homemade brush and powder to clean their teeth. It takes a while, but eventually, we enjoy the cleanest, most satisfied staff in the castle.

The maids are duty-bound to submit to Gwalchmei's advances whenever he chooses, but even he starts to notice the difference and begins bathing on a regular basis.

*

Now with hygiene improved, I turn my attention to nutrition. Not a lot of citrus fruits or bananas (i.e., none), but I find apples, pears, grapes, nuts, berries, and plenty of greens. In the event I ever return to civilization (or my time), I will be lucky to still hold a career, so I need to be in the best shape of my life to *earn* my spot back on the team. Something I haven't had to do in years.

With some borrowed woolen pants, I start running and working out. I was wearing some pretty decent kicks when I got clobbered, so I use those as running shoes, and just peel off my shirt. At first, the castle inhabitants assume I'm crazy, or worse, running from—or after—invisible spirits. A half-naked black man jogging laps around the castle in 523 AD., not something they see every day.

One of my first runs takes me back to where G found me. I am hoping to find a portal, spaceship, or *something* I could use to return my time. I see an old tree and some fallen branches. Not exactly a DeLorean.

My days consist of rising at dawn (say what you will, these people do *not* sleep in) to "breaking fast" with whatever fruits I can scrounge, time-managing the chores of the household staff, overseeing water and cleaning projects, lunch on leafy greens, and then a few hours of exercise. Gwalchmei's house is a picture of clockwork efficiency. If there was such a thing as clocks. Did I just invent the black butler? I am setting race relations back a hundred years, or forward fourteen hundred? Either way, I can pretty much stop expecting a Christmas card from the NAACP.

*

WE WILL NEVER BE ROYALS

The day of my Royal Audience arrives. I dress up in my original clothes. My jeans aren't tight when I tuck my nine in the back waistband, up under my jacket. My recent workouts and diet trimmed me down. Who am I kidding? I am in unbelievable shape. In just a few weeks, I dropped all the flab around my middle, and my muscle tone is denser than it was fifteen years ago.

I wear my twenty-first-century clothes for a reason. If my "in" with the King and Queen centers on the fact I'm something unique, then I am going to give them a show unlike any other. Gwalchmei coaches me on what to expect and how to act during the audience, and in turn, I tutor him on hygiene, nutrition, and some modern first-aid techniques. I spend my afternoons preparing. I will either become the next court jester,

155

end up running this place, or beheaded, but one way or the other, I am going to show them some shit they have never seen before.

*

When called in, Gwalchmei leads. The Royal Hall appears a noticeable step up from the rest of the castle. Polished marble and tapestries cover walls and floors alike. The guards at the door tell us it's standing room only. Few in the kingdom ever beheld a Moor before, let alone an enchanted one. The style of dress, materials, and thicker waistlines indicate this crowd fares much better than the common folk outside. More than clothing and jewelry, these people reek of entitlement. And they just plain reek. I would take the lowest servant of Gwalchmei's house staff over any one of these smelly snobs. G treats his crew fairly, but for the first time, the class segregation strikes me right between the eyes.

*

On Gwalchmei's cue, we both take a knee until addressed.

"Step forward, noble knight. Regale us with the tale of your capture of this creature," commands the blonde hotness on the throne. A bearded guy, with dirty blond hair, a little older than Gwalchmei, sits next to her on the larger throne. I'm no Sherlock Holmes, but I'm going to guess: The King.

"In truth, Your Highness, it was *he* who captured *me*. After a pitched battle lasting three days and three nights, this Moor defeated me through the use of great and powerful magicks."

Great and powerful magicks? I whupped him with stick in less than three seconds. Whatever.

An ancient turd of an old man steps up next to the King. "If this beq sooth, how do you both stand here?" He speaks at Gwalchmei, but his eyes never leave me.

"Ah, wise and wizened Myrddin, this Moor, named Henry of the House Morgan, granted my freedom and life and asked for naught, but my hand in friendship," Gwalchmei says.

"Methinks he be the loser of that exchange," Myrddin croaks.

With a sharp glance at the old man, the Queen continues, "Pray good knight, what magicks does this dark man demonstrate? We hear of many strange tales from your household. Surely, they be false."

"No, my Queen, in the fortnight since Friend Henry has taken residence in my meager home, my servants be happier, healthier, and with nary an instance of illness."

At this, the Queen sat up straighter. "You let a Moor sleep under your roof? How will you ever expel the fleas?"

Yeah. She said that. It was all I could do to keep my mouth shut, but G had explained to me how critical it is I not speak until spoken to. All this time, I didn't recognize what a real looker she is. Overwhelmed by the whole spectacle, I never noticed the age difference between her and the King. A girl, actually. Blonde, buxom, and so pale, she borders on translucent. Men in any century would consider her extraordinarily hot. Between her looks and the twinkle of intelligence in her eyes, it doesn't take the aforementioned Mr. Holmes to see the King is batting way out of his league.

Still, fleas? Really?

"To the contrary, my Queen. While his humanity may be in question, Henry here has purged my home magically of all pests and pestilence. His spells, which he names 'science,' cured my household of all its ills and he has beguiled even the lowest of my servants to bathe."

"Bathing? A clear sign of being in league with the Devil. Slay him before he can enthrall the Royal Court." Myrddin points both the index and pinkie fingers of one hand at me.

"Tell us, Henry of the House Morgan, use you *dark* magicks?" the King asks. This is the first time he spoke. And the first time anyone here spoke to me.

"Your Majesty," I say with a deep bow, just as rehearsed, "I do not use dark magicks, but common knowledge where I am from. I hail from a far-off land and wish nothing more than to return. But until then, I hope to use my knowledge for the benefit of your kingdom."

"Do you deny bewitching common folk into bathing, which all know as the Devil's welcome?" bellows Myrddin.

"I just convinced them they would not be as prone to illness if they bathed more. It doesn't hurt they also smell better. A lack of pain I heavily recommend. Even from here."

"Do not claim your dark arts more powerful than mine own gifts, monkey-man! An incubus sired me. I have been the Sorcerer Royale since before you were a swaddling," spit comes from Myrddin's lips as he screams. He is *pissed.*

"Actually, you weren't," Gwalchmei states flatly.

Myrddin wheels on the knight. "What! Of course I was! This ape-ling can be but a few decades in age, while I have presided as the King's wizard since His Majesty was but ten and three."

"But Henry of Morgan be thirty and six in years. And more. He conjures and speaks with spirits. He can count, read, and do mathematics. In his head," Gwalchmei says.

"NO! No man, and never a monkey-man, can do as you say! I, alone, age backward! Begone!" Myrddin is losing it. Waving his arms, a bloom of smoke puffs at my feet. All the bystanders step back in awe. "Hie ye away, DEVILSPAWN!"

There it is.

*

I glance at G. He gives me a slight signal, but looks really worried. I turn to the King. With a flourish, I bow low at the waist, never taking my eyes off the blond guy on the throne. "With permission, Your Majesties." He nods.

Batter up, bitch.

*

GOING TO THE SHOW

"Old man, I stood here politely while you called me a monkey-man, ape-ling, and devil spawn. Quite frankly, I have had about all of *that* shit I am going to take." Many gasp. It seems no one has ever talked back to him before. (And in an instant, I invent "uppity.") "Puffs of smoke ain't gonna cut it from here on in, Gandalf. Pal, give me something I can dance to, full volume."

Waves of bass thump from my chest. Background singers chime in. Electric guitar strains pierce the room. In case I hadn't mentioned it, the audio systems in the latest iPals are a thing of beauty. I would love to lecture you on all the cool micro-technology, but in reality, I don't know, nor care. All I know is: the sonic waves coming off that thing are so intense, my clothes actually vibrate.

To the room, it must appear as if I am summoning the music of Hell.

The entire room, Myrddin included, steps back. The King sits back in his throne, mouth open.

"Pal, play 'Amazing Grace,' full choir rendition, full volume."

Hearing the hymn's bagpipes, the King leans forward again. When the sisters in the choir kick in the vocals, the room belongs to me. I wait a moment after the song has finished before I speak again. I'm not a math wizard, but I know how to put on a show.

"Pal, what is 3,722 times 4,201?"

"*15,636,122,*" a female voice says, out of nowhere.

"Pal, who am I?"

"*You requested I refer to you as 'The Greatest Wizard on Earth.'*"

*

"ENOUGH! Sir Lancelot, strike down this speaker of demons! Slay him! NOW!" Myrddin screams.

A suit of armor, more massive than most, lurches toward me, sword in hand. G reaches for his weapon, but I put a hand on his shoulder to stop him. The King does not move to either stop or encourage the apparent slaying of the Greatest Wizard on Earth.

I speak to the knight in armor but am looking at Myrddin. "This will not end well for you."

I pull my nine millimeter and shoot Lancelot in the center of his chest.

A number of things happen simultaneously.

The impact knocks the knight in armor a foot off the floor, laying him out with a gigantic CLANG.

The crowd runs terrified for the exits, hearing the thunderclap of the gunfire and seeing the effects of the shot.

The King leaps to his feet, both hands on the arms of the throne.

The Queen puts her hand over her mouth and cries out.

Myrddin screams like a little girl.

That's my favorite part.

"G, with me." I move to the knight on the floor. Between us, we remove his chest piece. The hollow point round flattened on impact, on the outside of the steel plate. It leaves a fist-sized dent in his armor, a mighty bruise, and a few cracked ribs in its wake. I had a fifty-fifty chance it wouldn't penetrate. Luckily for both of us. Him, more than me, actually.

I turn to the throne.

"Your Majesty, I ... wait. '*Lancelot*?'" It's a statement, but it comes out as a question. I stare at Myrddin. "Then, he is ...?"

"The old wizard, who seems to have ... soiled himself?" Arthur says, somewhat amused.

"Gwalchmei called him Myrddin." I am having a hard time shifting gears here.

"Gwalchmei still clings to the old Welsh. Here, he answers to Sir Gawain. In Wales, Myrddin means Merlin."

"So, you must be ..."

"I am King Arthur, Lord of the Britains. To my left sits Milady Guinevere, and you've met Sir Lancelot."

Oh. And. Shit.

*

EXCUSE ME WHILE I WHIP THIS OUT

Merlin and most of the royal suck-ups disappear. Arthur, Guinevere, many of the knights, including Gawain, and I, talk till the wee hours.

"With what magical instrument did you best fair Lancelot?" asks the Queen.

I hold the Ruger up briefly. "This has many names, but many refer to it as a 'Nine.' Where I come from, people carry these for self-protection."

The Queen watches me tuck it into the back of my jeans.

"Any kingdom would be foolish of heart to attack a people with such magic," she says, looking at me.

"Yeah, and this one of the smallest."

Did no one else see her lick her lips?

*

At the end of the meeting, Arthur names me the new Sorcerer Royale.

"Merlin seems to hold that We don't comprehend that all his 'miracles' happen solely when no one can witness them. Through disguise and whispers, he manipulates and schemes. While you, black wizard, bested our finest with but a wave of your hand in Our Very Presence. You manifest voices and music from the ether. You are a true magician," Arthur states. "I bid you: use your magicks to raise Our kingdom to even loftier heights."

*

MAKING MAGIC

So I do. I expand my hygiene, nutrition, and exercise programs. It doesn't take long to transform Camelot into the healthiest, cleanest kingdom in the world.

With some technical advice from my iPal, I instigate irrigation, crop rotation, and selective breeding systems to enhance their farming.

I (and my iPal) "invent" manufacturing. From artillery weapons to clothing, to upgraded farm implements, to even paper production, we use assembly lines, blast furnaces, and spinning wheels to create better goods than the rest of the world will produce for centuries.

The Cameloteans ... the Arthurians ... whoever ... these folks aren't yet able to mine the mineral resources to manufacture gunpowder and build cannons, but I do teach them how to build trebuchets. This advances the castle's defenses nearly six hundred years ahead the rest of the world.

More importantly, I motivate Arthur's craftsmen to make some rudimentary gear, and I teach anyone who will listen the game of baseball. I need to keep my skills up. Arthur, in particular, loves the sport. In no time, baseball surpasses jousting in popularity since anyone can play it, from royalty to commoner. Soon, every village in the kingdom has a makeshift diamond. Now, *that's* what I call civilization.

I do experience a failure here and there. For the life of me, I cannot convince the knights to utilize guerrilla warfare. "'Tis dishonorable." Because lining up, charging into a fray, and getting slaughtered by the dozens is so much more honorable. What can you do against centuries of programming?

I keep a few agendas I don't exactly run past Arthur and the Church. First among these must be education. At this point in history, only priests and a few nobles can read. After swearing students to secrecy, I create underground schools and educate the peasants how to read, write, and do math. The writing exercises consist of copying primers to teach others. The Church has all the books—uh, Bibles. A few exceptional adult students, I push them to start their own schools. I encourage students mastering the basics to move on to more advanced studies, such as simple chemistry, alternate trade skills, and even rudimentary biology and medicine.

My education scheme is more than a little complicated as peasants must also perform their daily duties (in essence, slavery for the high-born) and not allowed to travel too far from their hovels. They must stop whatever they are doing to pray several times a day. For generations, the royals conditioned the peasants to see slaving for the nobility as an honor and God's Will.

Since I am re-inventing education, I decide to make this world a better place. I integrate accounting, business, technology (with my iPal's aid), social studies, and even race relations into the lessons. I invite the more curious of the students to touch my arm to show my skin, while darker, feels no different than theirs. I can't tell you how many times I prick my fingers to show them I bleed red too. Few of these people ever laid eyes on a black man and all they know springs from superstition, fear, and ignorance. I am determined to enlighten them.

Along with teaching racial equality, I try to imbue to the male students the essence of how a real man should act. But it's the sixth century, and my gender-related lessons seem to fall on deaf ears. Hopefully, some of them get it.

While secretly teaching the masses, I too, learn more than I suspected. Many a late night I spend with Arthur discussing honor, leadership, humility, and statesmanship. From Gawain and Knights of the Round Table, I learn duty, loyalty, camaraderie, and fidelity. I don't imagine how soon I will find those lessons useful.

All goes pretty much as planned. Arthur delegates a humble staff of servants to me, who, after some private education, I promote to 'middle management,' supervising my various improvement projects. Manufacturing, defensive measures, hygiene, health, and quality of life soar to an all-time high. The underground schools churn out more enlightened graduates each day, reducing the gap between nobles and peasants.

Right about then, the summons arrives to attend the Queen's chambers.

*

THE QUEEN'S WEAPON OF CHOICE

"Henry of the House Morgan," she begins, "I would have you tell me of your world. Have you a bride? Does your kind even marry?"

"Yes, Your Majesty, my 'kind' does marry, and I am. Mrs. Morgan and I don't see each other much, probably why we're still together. We have an understanding. I understand if she catches me, I'm a dead man." An old joke, but for some reason, I'm nervous and trying to break the tension.

"That I DO understand. So. Moorish men and women have relations, just as we do here?"

"I don't know any Moors. I'm from New York, and I don't know relations from relativity here. Been a tad busy," I reply.

"Have you not taken a woman since your arrival? Gawain's maids and mine own eyes tell me you are larger than the men of our kingdom. Perhaps there lies the reason."

She's right there. I am at least six to eight inches taller than all the men of this era, except for Lancelot, and he has just a few inches on me. Wait. Did she say Gawain's maids? Why would ... Oh. And. Shit.

"Show me your 'Nine,'" she commands.

"What?"

"Your weapon. Pull out your weapon."

"Your Majesty, I don't think I should ..."

"Henry of Morgan, I desire to see the weapon that bested Sir Lancelot."

"Oh." I reach behind me and pull out the Ruger.

"Come closer so I may touch it."

I eject the round in the chamber, re-engage the safety, pop the clip, and step forward to hold the empty gun to her.

She grabs my crotch.

"This DOES best Sir Lancelot."

I jump back several paces. I'm shocked. Not just at her actions, but at my own.

"Your Majesty! I can't believe I'm saying this, but as gorgeous as you are, and frankly, as much as I would enjoy it, I *am* married. Maybe this place is rubbing off on me, but I guess an oath should mean something. I hope you understand."

"Ah, Black Wizard, I fear you do not. Whoever holds such a weapon, can rule the world. I intend to possess it. One way or the other. I will hold your Moorish weapon in my hand."

To say I couldn't escape her rooms fast enough qualifies as a monstrous understatement. I'm still backing up well into the hall. Slamming right into a waiting Merlin.

"Enjoy your audience with Her Majesty, Friend Morgan?" the old wizard asks, straightening my jacket and vest. "You appear ... bothered. Most find a visit to Her Majesty's chambers ... invigorating."

"Well, the Queen does give good conversation. Sorry, Gandalf old boy, but I need to go. So many illusions, so little time. You know how busy it is being the King's sorcerer and all. I mean, you used to."

"Yes, Friend Morgan," he whispers. "I do."

*

THE PURLOINED PAL

That sonuvabitch! He lifted my iPal. I was so flummoxed from my audience with the Queen, I all but handed it to him. I need to speak with Arthur. Now.

*

"What proof do you offer the old man stole your magic slate?" His Majesty asks. "A trickster and charlatan, yes, but he has never sunk to thievery."

I explain what's going to happen. "Your Majesty, I propose we ride to Merlin's tower, we shall see, or rather, hear, for ourselves."

*

Our entourage approaches, and even a few dozen meters from Merlin's tower we hear the klaxon echoing from the stone walls.

Arthur looks at me aghast and with a touch of sadness. He turns in the saddle to his guards. "Arrest Merlin. Do not harm him. Touch not what you find there."

*

As they hold Merlin bound and gagged, I pick up the blaring device. "Pal, unlock." The voice and facial recognition and fingerprint scanner disengage the alarm. Arthur strides away from the tower without a glance back.

*

Arthur does not order Merlin's imprisonment or execution, as much out of nostalgia as anything. He strips the old man of any titles, lands, position, and exile him to the life of a commoner. For someone of Merlin's nature, it may have been more merciful to kill him.

*

JOUST IN TIME

"I challenge thee, Moor." Lancelot bellows.

"For the last time, I am not a—oh, forget it."

"I will not allow you to besmirch Her Majesty's honor. I hear gossip that you, a sub-human ape-ling, has had relations with Her Majesty. It is beyond tolerance."

Ape-ling? This starts to ring a little familiar. Plus, who knows I had a private audience with the Queen? I'm going out on a limb.

"What's Merlin feeding you, Lance?"

"'Tis true, the wizened one spoke to me, but with mine own eyes, I see how she looks at you. Most likely, you ensorcelled her affections. You will answer for your perfidy. Choose your weapon, monkey-man."

"Okay. I choose nine millimeters."

"Alas, I do not possess 'nine millimeters.'"

"Yeah. Sorry about that." In reality, I'm not.

"Choose again."

I mull it over. I need to eliminate any of his advantages. "Well, I don't own a sword, so if we must do this, let's fight hand-to-hand."

"Nay, 'tis unseemly. Hastilude in the lists. The next tournament sets but a fortnight away. My varlets will supply you with a charger and suitable accoutrements," Lancelot announces, turning to leave.

"Hastilude?" I ask Gawain.

"Jousting."

Phenomenal. In two weeks I need to learn how to beat a guy in an event in which he is undefeated. No problem. Now, all I need to do is invent the DeLorean.

*

Gawain offers to teach me jousting, and while I manage the lance, I can't get the hang of riding on horseback.

No. If I am to survive this insanity, I need to think outside the box. Given these people don't even own boxes; how hard can it be? With iPal in hand, I move into Merlin's vacated tower.

*

The night before the joust, a few peasants collect Lancelot's armor, saddle, and his horse's armaments for polishing. Lancelot doesn't give them a second look, and his personal squires rejoice with the reduced labor.

The next morning, I watch as they lower Lancelot on to his horse.

"Squire, why does my armor glisten so? Who cleaned it? Why does my mount's armor not shine as well?"

"Peasants, milord, from the castle. Ones never seen before. As to the horse's armor, they thought you would prefer the Royal Eyes solely on you."

"Find out the secret to the polish. I would'st all my armor sparkle so at every occasion. You say you don't know them?" Lancelot looks in my direction, eyes narrowed. "Make secure the bindings, as well ensure all is in working order. I trust not this black fiend."

"Yes, milord. We were suspicious as well and checked the armor thoroughly. It will work as never before."

He got that right.

*

Lancelot rides slowly to one end of the lists. I walk to the other. His armor glistens in the sun. My twenty-first-century apparel shocks all in attendance.

"Friend Henry, I implore thee. Don armor at least," Gawain begs. "Lancelot will slay thee in a single ride. His lance be not blunted. Without armor, he will pierce thine heart in his first pass."

"G, with any luck at all, Lance won't even come close," I reply, not sure who I'm trying to convince. Gawain sure as hell isn't buying. Time for me to give one last try.

I yell down the lists, "Lancelot, any chance if I ask you not to do this, you would pass? For your own sake?"

"Prepare to die, black dog of Hell." Well, as long as he's conflicted about it.

We both salute the King.

Lancelot kicks his steed to a bouncing gallop toward me. I step forward, hands spread wide and empty in the air. I see what I am waiting for and yell, "SHAZAM!"

Hey, it's the sixth century. I don't need to be original.

Lancelot's suit of armor explodes into flame.

Merlin runs toward his champion as fast as his ancient legs will carry him, grabbing a bucket on the way.

I see his intent in an instant and yell, "Not water!"

When the bucket of water hits Lancelot, the flames spread farther.

I grab the bucket from the old wizard and fill it with sand and dirt from the lists. Bucket after bucket I toss on Lancelot. I finally smother the fire.

Taking off my jacket, I wrap my hands in it to extract Lancelot out of his armor. Layers of chain mail helped protect him, but he will be looking at living with some nasty burns. Squires take him off the field, and Gawain follows them, utilizing some of my first aid training. Guinevere follows them in tears. A few too many tears.

Merlin stands in awe and confusion. Arthur looks at me.

"Wizard Henry, how did you set brave Lancelot aflame with a wave of your hand? A blaze Merlin could not quench?" Even Merlin looks at me for the answer.

"Science, Your Majesty." I'm not feeling exceptionally heroic. I just set one of history's bravest knights on fire. Now granted, it beats the hell out of him puncturing me with that oversized stick, but I am still not too proud of myself. What I'm *not* telling Arthur is the night before, I had some of my students polish Lancelot's armor with a waxy gel, similar to Napalm mixed with gelignite, created with the help of my iPal. Camelot doesn't own sufficient quantities of the right minerals to use this technology in defense of Camelot, but Merlin's tower has the proper ingredients, plus whatever Pal instructed my students to find in nature, to coat a suit of armor. When cleaning Lancelot's gear, they swapped several ornamental pieces on the saddle with similar ones, made of roughened quartz. When Lancelot's armor bounced up and down in the saddle, it scratched the flint creating the spark igniting the Napalm-like coating of his armament. His chain mail would have protected him, if not for Merlin's water seeping into the crevices.

*

WHO DA HO?

Life never fails to surprise you. I'm back in time fifteen hundred years. I outwitted Merlin the Magician (twice), defeated the greatest knight ever born (twice), dodged the clutches of a power-hungry, nymphomaniac, adulteress queen, and became the second most powerful person in Europe. Oh yeah—and singlehandedly changed civilization. One would assume I would be blessed with the smarts to stop there. Go figure.

I ask to speak to Arthur alone. I'm struggling with whether or not to break it to him His Queen is an unfaithful ho. Not something you tell the King of all the Britains every day. Or, you know ... ever.

I try to speak with Gawain on the subject, but he slams his fist into the table and stomps from the room. Evidently, royal infidelity, not a subject he warms to.

The day of my appointment with Arthur arrives, and we sit at a modest, but not round, table.

I ask about the Queen. I ask how Lancelot's doing. I try as diplomatically as possible to communicate the point. As a diplomat, I make a phenomenal catcher.

The last thing I see before the lights fade: a tarnished signet ring. Real, real close.

*

BACK TO THE FUTURE MCFLY

My head hurts. Stop with the shaking already. Did I mention my head hurts?

"Hank, you okay buddy?" Artie asks, genuine concern in his voice. I manage to force my eyes open into some retina-burning stadium lighting. Artie looms over me, close enough to kiss me. His face a mask of concern.

"What happened?" I manage to mutter.

"Wow. You really got nailed. It's top of the eighth, and France's pitcher figures you less of threat on first than busting the fence. So he beaned you." By now, Coach and the umpire stand over me.

"I guess that's one way to keep a brother down," I murmur.

"Whoa, son," the umpire says. "I don't know where that kind of talk came from, but I'm writing it off to a hit to the head. There's no need for racist trash talk in His Majesty's Baseball League. Go sit down."

"I'm good. Help me up," I say. Coach sends a designated runner to first and the crowd cheers as I am half-carried to the dugout. I study the lineup. "Where's L?"

"Hank, maybe we do need to have you checked out." Artie looks into my eyes for signs of concussion. "L passed years ago. You know that."

"What?"

"Yeah, man. Swallowed his nine. Guess he just couldn't stand folks finding out." Artie hangs his head down, his voice a mere whisper. He lowers me to the bench. "Being gay—well, he couldn't take it and just took the off-ramp."

"But, Artie, aren't you ...";

"WHAT!? What're you gonna say, Hank? I got two kids and an ex-wife. I'm a world-class athlete, play the most popular sport in the world, and am winning the World Friggin' Series. What're you gonna ask, Hank?"

The World Series? Oh. And. Shit!

*

I spy the scoreboard. I grab Artie's jersey. "Is that the score? I need an iPal. Right. Now!"

A batboy hustles mine from the locker room. "Pal, call Rudy." I walk to the far end of the dugout.

"Rudy, it's Hank. Tell-me-you-didn't-place-the-bet." I snap at the image on the screen.

"Hank, calm down. You okay? I saw that beaner on TV. He genuinely nailed you, and then some." Rudy seems more ... together than ever before. Is he wearing a tie?

"I'm fine. Rudy, I just saw the scoreboard. We carry a five-run lead. Tell me you didn't place that bet." I am now pleading.

"Henry, first of all, you know damned well I'm a stockbroker and not a bookie. Secondly, you know baseball is all but cheat-proof. You couldn't bet on it if you wanted to. And thirdly, what the hell are you talking about?"

"Thank God." I am not sure if I feel more relief he didn't place the bet or that I didn't. I can't conceive I ever wished to.

*

We win the World Series. Reporters. Champagne. I go through the motions of dressing in a fog. Was it all a dream?

I contemplate the locker room. The average physiques of ballplayers that I am used to seeing now display chiseled abs and zero body fat. So. Not a dream.

After the other players have left to celebrate, Artie and I sit in the locker room.

"Hank, I'm sorry about going all medieval on you out there. I don't know what gets into me."

"Artie, don't give it a thought. I guess I'm a little fuzzy. You know I'm gonna love you like a brother no matter what, right?"

"I know," Artie's eyes well up a bit. "I thought that was cool you telling that reporter it was a team effort. Not your usual style at all."

"Maybe I've learned a few things lately. You know, grown as a human being. Learned some humility, or honor. Become a real man. Or ... maybe that shot to the head was harder than I thought." I finally score a smile.

Artie looks at the clock. "Grab your gear. Isn't your gorgeous girlfriend coming by in a few to pick you up?"

"Girlfriend? You mean *Trish*?" Artie knows I'm *married* to the Bitch from Hell. For years now.

"Trish? That goose egg on your swollen melon will acquire a twin if you call Gwen some other chick's name."

*

I pack my personal stuff in a duffle. I start to slip my iPal into my bag. It's thinner and lighter than I remember. Thinking back on it, the picture resolution's much higher as well. I flip it over. On the back, etched into the aluminum case, a logo of a sword coming out of a stone.

*

EXCERPTS FROM QUESTIONING IPAL:

"Racial differences stopped factoring into societal interactions in the seventh century."

"Masculinity, fidelity, and honor remain highly revered characteristics in male behavior."

"Homosexuality is a criminal, moral, and ethical offense. The authorities prosecute alternate sexual orientations to the fullest extent of the law. See HM Penal Code 514.297"

"Great Britain conquered the majority of the civilized world in the ninth century and has since led the globe in technology, education, social reform, and baseball."

"No records found for 'the Revolutionary War,' 'Civil War,' or 'Declaration of Independence.'"

"Fitness and nutrition are at all-time highs with less than one-one hundredth of one percent of the population struggling with obesity or malnutrition."

"Baseball is the most popular sport in the world. Every nation on Earth competes in The World Series (see His Majesty's Baseball League *for more information). More money is spent on advertising in baseball than all other sports combined. Fan attendance dwarfs any other sporting event."*

"Football, hockey, soccer, and Olympic sports rank behind professional bowling and polo in popularity."

"No records found for the terms 'basketball' or 'NBA.'"

***

The Bet

Immortal entities wager on a man's choice of life or death.

So. Life and Death walk into a bar. Well, not really a bar. On the ethereal plane, it is the metaphysical equivalent of sitting down with a glass of scotch and good cigar. But the view is spectacular.

"How's business?" asks Life. "Wait, never mind. Every time I lose one, you gain one. Our numbers should be identical."

"Except I always get the last laugh," smirks Death. "What do you think about that guy?"

"Which one?"

"That one there," pointing his spiritual finger.

"Oh, I see him," Life says. "Seems like he's doing okay. Beautiful apartment, gorgeous girlfriend. He is definitely enjoying me."

"Seems a little despondent, if you ask me. Looks like I might get another one sooner than later."

Life stares intently at the man on the mortal plane. "He'll be fine."

"You think? Let's watch. I have a good feeling about him."

*

David is cleaning his overpriced penthouse when he sees it.

"Damn. She forgot her phone." The phone is unlocked and as he picks it up, the screen displays her text app. She must have been using it very recently.

His face pales as he reads the sexually explicit texts on it. He doesn't hear the elevator door to their apartment open as Jezzabelle breezes into the main room, stepping down the two marble steps from the elevator foyer. Her red mini-dress displaying ample cleavage, midriff, and leg as she looks up from digging through her matching red purse.

"Hi David, It's me. I forgot my—" She stops when she sees his expression and what he is holding.

"What ... what is this?" he stammers.

"It's my private property and you have no business looking at it," she says coolly.

"Technically, it's mine. I pay the bills. Who is Mortey?"

"Nice. Isn't that just like you to throw it in my face that you pay the phone bill," Jezzabelle glares.

"I pay ALL the damned bills. Whatever. I'm sorry I looked at *your* phone. Who's Mortey?"

"He's just a guy I met. He's nice. There's absolutely nothing between us."

"Really?" his face reddening as he grips the phone tighter. "These texts are pretty suggestive for *nothing.*"

"You're reading too much into it. Mortey's just a nice guy."

"Jez, he talks about how *good* you were the other night. That's more than just a guy you met," David's voice cracks as he speaks. "He's looking forward to being with you in just little bit."

"He treats me nice," Jezzabelle says. "Like you used to."

"Like I used to? What do you think this apartment is? For pity's sake, I paid for your boob job."

176

"Well, I needed them for my career. Do you want them back? Tough. You were a different man when you had a job," she says as she snatches the phone from his hand.

"So, it's my fault the market tanked? And what career? You haven't had a modeling gig in months. Unless you call power shopping a career now," David lashes out at the gorgeous redhead.

"And whose fault is it that I haven't worked, David? I begged you to let me get my lips and cheek bones done, but you refused. I would be on a runway right now if it wasn't for your stinginess. 'Jezzabelle' would be a household word."

"Stinginess? I took a bath unloading my stocks and even cashed out my retirement plan just to keep you in style. I am all but broke. Would Mortey do that for you?"

"He wouldn't have to. He is independently wealthy and treats me like a lady."

"What kind of name is *Mortey*, anyway? Seems a little goofy, like a friggin' Disney character," the pettiness coming out in his voice.

"He says it's an old family name. I think he's from Europe. He's very gallant and doesn't throw his money in my face. I love how understated he is. He takes me for drives in his '67 Mustang. It's off-white and when he puts the top down, I feel so alive."

*

Life looks at Death. "A pale Mustang? Really, *Mortey*?

Death shrugs. "Hey, you know me. I'm a big fan of the classics. What can I say? No one compelled her to go. Not exactly a kidnap victim, if you know what I mean."

*

David paces the room. He stares at the infrequently used kitchen with its state-of-the-art appliances. The surfaces gleam like they did in the showroom. He looks at the designer furniture. Uncomfortable and uninviting, but nearly artistic in their form. Her jasmine perfume lingers everywhere. He looks around for anything to keep from looking at her and her phone. He picks up a Rutherford vase and stares at it. He marvels at the weight of it. They must have priced it by the pound.

"Aren't we in love?" the anguish in his voice the total opposite of the frigid tone in hers.

"I may have loved you ... once. But since you lost your job, you're half the man you used to be."

"This whole time ... our life together ... has been nothing but a lie?"

Jezzabelle walks to a wall mirror to check her perfect red lipstick. "Not the whole time. We had some fun, didn't we? I mean, at first."

"So that's it then?" David asks. "I run out of money, you decide you don't love me, and now you run to Mortey?"

"Well, to be honest, it didn't happen exactly in that order, and I am not running to anyone in these heels, but yes, I am going to be with Mortey now."

"GO BE WITH MORTEY THEN, BITCH!" David hurls the vase in Jezzabelle's direction. Even blinded by rage and frustration, he deliberately misses her. Jez dodges the crystal as it smashes into the elevator door, but falls, unable to keep her footing in heels. Her head sounds an audible crack as it impacts the edge of the marble step.

David races to her limp form. Kneeling beside her body, hands out, afraid to touch her.

"Oh, Jez. What have I done?" He watches the rivulet of blood slipping down to the next step like a liquid Slinky. Her eyes stare blankly, as if surprised that this could happen to her.

*

Death does a pitch perfect Tim Curry imitation, "One for the vaults."

"We're not watching her," says Life. "We are discussing him. I'm sure he'll recover from this. It was an accident. The authorities will vindicate him. Without her to spend his money and cheat on him, he will probably thrive."

"Self-delusion is just another form of lying, brother," Death replies. "Keep watching. Excuse me while I go use the Little Entities' Room."

*

"What'll it be, boyo?"

David looks up to find himself seated at a bar. The smell of old oak and stale beer assaults his senses. The mirror behind the bar reflects a zombified version of himself. He doesn't remember getting here, but is not surprised. His life has become a walking nightmare.

"Are ye langered, lad?" the bartender asks.

"What?"

"Langered. Lashed. You know ... drunk?" The bartender glares at David while wiping down the bar.

"No, no. Uh, give me a Jameson's."

"Aye." Sitting the glass in front of David, "That'll be $8.50."

David slides his Amex from his wallet and across the bar. "Start a tab, would you ...?" He squints at the barkeep's name badge.

"Fírinne. It's Irish for 'truth,'" the bartender explains. "Me sainted Pap had a sense of humor naming me Fírinne, as me older brother was a rale Bulgarian and a chancer of epic proportions. Everyone just calls me Fear." The bartender explains as he runs the credit card.

"A chancer?"

"Aye, a big, fat liar. A rale Bulgarian is what ye might call an uncivilized lout." The bartender turns to David. "Laddie, I'm gonna need to be seeing some cash for the nip. The credit card company not only declined this card, but told me to destroy it."

"That card *has* to be good. Try this one."

"Nay, lad. I'll be seeing some cash, or ye'll be going thirsty." The barkeep pulls the glass back from David's hand.

"Keep your stupid drink," David snaps as he storms out the door into the night.

179

The barkeep smiles, looks at the glass, and then at the door. "Well, we won't be getting that back into the bottle now, will we?" He swallows the drink in one gulp.

*

Life glares at Death as he returns. "I am *not* fat."

Death smiles mischievously, "That's okay. There's no such thing as a Little Entities' Room either."

"David is going to get it together," Life says. "Look, he's going to a church. That has to be a good sign." Life fixes his glare on Death, "You stay right here. No more interfering."

"Aye, laddie. Nary a shenanigan from me. This is all up to Him now."

*

The door is locked. David beats on it. *Even God's house is afraid of late-night vandals, I guess.* He slumps, sitting on the step. *Maybe this is close enough for Him to hear me.* He bows his head, clasps his hands, whispering solemnly.

"God, please fix this. Everything is so horrible now. You can do this. You can make everything right again. I'm begging You. Talk to me. Tell me everything will be fine."

David waits.

The only sound was an ambulance siren blocks away.

David sits and waits for an answer. After a while, not even conscious of doing it, he drives away in a car he can no longer afford.

*

"You knew there would be no answer," Life accuses Death.

"Yeah, that's not how Dad rolls."

"David will still choose life. He has everything to live for. This can be a new beginning for him," Life maintains.

Death watches as the morning sun finds David as he steps closer to the edge of the cliff.

"Wanna bet?"

***

The Fall

On the cliff's edge of suicide, a mortal questions
God's power.

Certainly, the fall will kill me. The grassy floor of the cliff rests a hundred feet below. As I stand inches from the edge, dirt crumbles under my shoes tumbling toward the bottom. "Precipice." That's what they call it. A fancy word for lots of empty air punctuated by hardened earth. I raise my left foot as if to step out into the Nothing when a glowing ball of energy coalesces in front me. Out over the edge of the cliff in midair.

What the hell? It swirls like a dense, circular cloud of blue, twinkling stars, in broad daylight. Well, broad-ish. A beautiful dawn sky breaks oranges and reds.

"Hello, David." The voice in my head is almost deafening. Although, I somehow know it's some sort of telepathy, I instinctively clasp my hands over my ears.

"Who ... who ... WHAT are you?" I yell, compensating for the volume in my head.

"Who do you think I am?"

"I don't know. An alien?"

"That's a good one. No. I was here long before what humans call aliens showed up. One could say, I was responsible for the human race as it is."

"Are you ... God?"

"Straight for the metaphysical. I like it. Shows some imagination. Here's what we'll do. Let's play a game."

"A game? Seriously? You want to play games with me? I must be hallucinating all this. I've lost my job. I lost my wife. My life is a complete disaster and now I have lost my mind once and for all."

"Oh, for the love of Me, stop whining. Your life wasn't so bad. You are not crazy. Well, not any crazier than the rest of humanity, at least. How about this? Ask twenty questions and I will answer. If you arrive at the right conclusions, I will fix your life. Deal?"

"Do I have a choice?"

"Yes, of course. Free will and all that. Would you like to play a game?"

"I guess. I definitely need someone to fix my life. But quoting *War Games*, seriously?"

"Yes. Great flick. Way deeper than Ferris Bueller. And we're off with question number one."

"No. Wait. How does that count?"

"Because we started playing once you agreed, and then you formed a sentence with a question mark at the end. Am I going too fast? That's question number two, by the way. Screaming is not necessary. I can hear your thoughts just fine."

"Yeah, about that. Why are You speaking English? Shouldn't it be Hebrew or Aramaic or something?"

"I am actually not speaking anything. Your brain is translating the impulses I am sending as English. And doesn't it make sense I would know ALL languages? Those were questions three and four. I wish I could cut you some slack, but rules are rules."

"If this isn't some sort of prank, then why sound like Morgan Freeman?"

"Because, in your mind, the voice of God should sound like Morgan Freeman. David, David, David, question number five. Twenty-five percent of the way done. Isn't it time for the really big questions?"

"Okay. You want big, I can do big. Why do You let all the wars, crime, and evil happen in the world?"

"That's more like it. I, personally, don't let evil happen. People have free will. Mankind does those things all on its own. Would mindless slavery be better?"

"What about disease and pain and suffering? We don't choose those."

"That's true. These are some good ones. As cruel as it may seem, the bad things are there so mortals can appreciate the good things, like health, joy, and love. It's all part of the big picture."

"Sounds like a bit of a cop-out. What about answering prayers?" I fume over all the prayers I wasted about her and I getting back together.

"I don't do prayers. Oh, once in a great while, I might indulge Myself in a few guilty pleasures, but very rarely. Imagine this: an omnipotent Entity creates a matrix for the universe, all universes actually. This program is so complex it contains the orbital paths of galaxies, gravity, time, energy, matter, atomic weights, individual snowflakes, DNA coding, even Matthew Broderick. The program is then compiled, started, and launched, doing as it will, with the wild card of free will thrown in. Would an Entity working on that scale have the time or inclination for replying to individual requests?"

"God doesn't do prayers? Sure doesn't sound like any God I've heard of. The Bible, and almost every scriptural text I've ever heard of, says He answers our prayers. Why else would we spend so much time praying?"

"No, as before, I don't answer prayers. A repeat question? As for spending time praying, I don't think most people are praying to Me actually. Could it be they are in reality trying to connect with something bigger so they feel better about themselves? Two more questions down by the way."

"How many questions do I have left?"

"Counting that one, nine. I can't believe a mortal is having this conversation and wasting opportunities like they were nothing. And not for nothing, but I know about Nothing. I was there when it was."

He's right. I am wasting questions. I need to think this through. There's an opportunity here to change not just MY life, but everyone's. "What question can I ask where the answer would give me the knowledge to improve the life of every person on Earth?"

"None really. The formula for free, limitless energy would destroy the lives of the oil barons. Peace on earth would mess with manufacturers, warlords, military personnel, politicians, and activists. There is no making EVERYONE happy. Question number twelve, for the record."

"Oh, come on! I didn't even ask that; I was thinking it. How is that fair?"

"Seriously, another one? Okay. I said I would answer all twenty questions. It's fair because earlier I stated clearly, I was reading your thoughts. It still amazes me humans are at the top of the food chain. Should have been dolphins."

"What can mankind do about surviving and thriving?"

"Nice. Broad-based, altruistic, a real Jimmy Stewart thing going there. The answer is: nothing. I have looked at all the various timelines and mankind always becomes extinct. It may be in a year or it may be in a million millennia, but eventually mankind screws up. Reminds Me of a quote from a journalist, 'Never take life seriously. Nobody gets out alive anyway.' Same guy said in response to 'Life is hard,' 'Compared to what?' Funny guy. Bottom line: humans will someday die off."

Strange, He can depress a person on the edge of suicide even more. Maybe I am shooting too big. Maybe I should take this down to a more personal level.

"Why doesn't she love me anymore?"

"Tough one. I like it. Love is caring more about someone or something than yourself. Living with you became so toxic, manic, and depressing for her, she protected herself emotionally by leaving. By caring more about her own personal needs and psychological health than yours, she shifted her love to herself. Or maybe she was never truly in love to

184

begin with. Or maybe there is no such thing as love. I can go a number of ways on this one."

"NO LOVE? Are You kidding me? God is the embodiment of love. How can You say that?"

"No, I am not kidding you. As I noted earlier, neither am I 'saying' it. I project it. Be that as it may, after the launch of the initial programming of Everything, even I am not one hundred percent sure whether love exists or is a chemical reaction, or a self-generated psychological need. I believe I was loved once, but even I may have deluded Myself."

"So we shouldn't believe in the Bible?"

"David, one shouldn't believe in things if they DON'T exist. The Bible physically exists. Your mother has one. Of course, everyone should believe in it. There's one sitting on her nightstand."

"How can I fix my life?"

"Sorry, you can't."

"What's that mean? Just like that, 'I can't'? Even The Almighty is giving up on me?

"We have reached the end of our game. Your twenty questions are up. What conclusions did you arrive at? If you are correct, I will fix your life."

I give it some thought. The anger and frustration from this encounter have given me a new determination to live. But not before I vent.

"Okay. For almost my whole life I didn't believe You existed, but now I do. And I am pissed off. You are God, a spiteful, petty tyrant not caring about anyone but Himself. No matter what You say, I don't need you to fix my life, I *am* going to fix it on my own and win her back."

"AANNNH! Thanks for playing, David. But you are wrong on almost every count. I am not God. I believe I am about as close as one can come to Him though, even if I do say so Myself. I never said I was the Omnipotent Entity. Think about it. Why would I appear when the morning star came up? Nothing? Here's a clue: My Divinity was so impressive, He felt threatened and kicked me out of My Home. Wow. Dense, much?

"Once we started playing the game, you never once asked me who I am. One simple question would have saved yourself a whole lot of pain. I sound like Morgan Freeman because EVERYONE thinks that's what the voice of God should sound like. It was your preconceived assumption I was God. You should have asked what would happen if you lost the game before we started. Big mistake. It was deliriously easy pushing your buttons, inciting emotional, stupid questions. Even though you have exceeded your allotted twenty questions, I'm feeling generous. At this point, I have nothing to lose.

"I did NOT give up on you. I have worked keeping your life going longer than your body should have been able to withstand. It has taken but a few seconds to play our little game.

"There is no winning her back and you can't fix your life, David, because it's over. Open your eyes. You have been lying at the bottom of the cliff this whole time."

I look up. The cliff wall towers above me as everything fades to black.

"The good news is: we'll be seeing each other again real soon."

***

Carefree

A motorcyclist's worries fly away while rolling

Carefree. That's how he envisioned bikers as a kid from the back of his parents' station wagon. *Free as the wind, blasting down the highway, swerving in and out of traffic, without a worry in the world.* He longed to be grown up enough to own a motorcycle and experience true freedom. He couldn't wait for such carefree abandonment, with no homework, girls, parents, or ANYTHING to weigh him down. That would be the life!

(Puff!)

He reminisces back to his teens, borrowing his friends' dirt bikes, worrying that if he broke them, he couldn't afford to fix or replace them. Eventually, he struggled and scraped to buy his own, albeit used, Honda 450cc Nighthawk. It was all he could afford, mowing grass and working part-time for a construction contractor after school. As much as he cherished his Nighthawk, it didn't satisfy his needs. He ached for a big bike to transport him and his cares effortlessly down rural byways in a Peter-Fonda-esque blur.

Man, I need to slow it down a bit. This bend is a perfect place for a deer to jump out of the brush. When I crest this hill, what's on the other side: a line of traffic at a standstill or a sudden turn? Do I have enough gas to limp to the next service station? I need to remember to check my chain when I get home. Is it going to rain?

(Puff!)

As he neared high school's end, he sold the 450 to help pay for his upcoming tuition. His father passed away a few years prior, and his mother squirreled away the meager life insurance money available to them, to finance his way through college. He sold anything he owned of any value, including his treasured Nighthawk. It crumbled the edges of his heart to do it, but he needed every nickel to afford school. He continued to labor part time in construction while attending day and evening classes at the local community college, helping his mother as much as possible. His height and size landed him a job on weekends as a bouncer. The contractor work, a yard-sale set of weights, and his father's genes gave him the physique of a bodybuilder. But athletics never interested him. Running with a football never gave him the thrill of straightening the curves of the Blue Ridge Parkway. Not a week passed in which the road warrior in him didn't yearn to put his "knees in the wind" once more.

How can I afford a bike? I need to work at least one or two more jobs per week to afford it. Mom needs even more help with the rent. What if I talk to my boss at the bar about more hours? When I do get a bike, how much will it cost to maintain it?

(Puff!)

With a commercial art degree in hand, he snared a job as an assistant art director for a small ad agency. Although thankful for gainful employment, no one would describe his art director salary as astronomical. Despite his working multiple jobs throughout school and the limited help his mother could provide, he had accumulated what seemed a crushing mountain of debt from tuition and books. To add to his worries, his mother was getting on in years, and he continued to live at home to help her financially and physically around their small, two-bedroom bungalow.

A year out of college, he had scrimped enough to place a down payment on a Harley Davidson Road King. Several years old, but as clean as the day it came off the assembly line, the Harley called to him. It would require working two or three jobs for several years. He became desperate to find regular freelance jobs to help make the nut, but he now owned a REAL bike. His mother pestered him until he agreed to take the AMA motorcycle safety course, with a certain amount of reluctance, even though he already had his motorcycle endorsement from his Nighthawk days. Upon completing the three-day course, he realized it had knocked the rust off of some of his old skills and in truth, he learned a few new things to make him a safer rider.

And ride he did. Without exception, each moment not working or helping out at home, he rode. His co-workers thought of him as *eccentric* for always riding his motorcycle to work. He took every precaution: checking its tires on a regular basis (a blowout at sixty miles per hour could put a real crimp in your day), filling any fluids as needed, inspecting his tires daily for tread depth. He wore a Kevlar-armored jacket and pants, and always wore his helmet, though the state did not require one over the age of twenty-one. He ached for the peace of mind and freedom nothing but the open road could give him.

Whoa! Where did that BMW come from? Oh. Texting while driving. Damned kids will be the death of me. Okay, maybe she is just a few years younger than I am. Checking over my shoulder twice to make sure a semi changing lanes doesn't crush me like a beer can. Triple checking the mirrors. You just can't be too sure. Gotta keep scanning the road for debris.

(Puff!)

He remembers worrying about needing to build a shed large enough to keep his bike out of the elements. Later, when his mother could no longer drive, he held on to their old family car, to ferry her to her treatments and run errands for her, but vowed never to be dependent on four wheels himself.

Is that car going to come to a complete stop at the intersection? Do I have enough tread on my tires to pass inspection? What if a dog ran out in front of me right now?

On his first vacation from the agency, he rode his motorcycle to Sturgis Bike Week in South Dakota. He had pinched pennies for more than a year, skipping lunches and living like a miser to afford the camping trip. The ride itself took up most of his time off, and he spent very little actual time in Sturgis itself. Punctuated with the stress of riding racetrack-like slabs of highway, the heavy traffic he encountered, the threat of running out of gas, the possibility of the bike breaking down, and areas where his cell phone had no signal, the entire trip had exhausted him with a general sense of tension and strain.

Damn! Soccer mom fussing with a van full of kids turned left on me! My front tire is going to need to be replaced soon if I keep locking them up like that. Reminds me of the weekend a biker in Daytona swerved out in front me during Bike Week. Surviving involved a matter of inches, lightning reflexes and good luck.

All these memories flood through him as his mom arrives home, bone tired and weary. Her bus stop is a long walk from their home, and the chemotherapy is poisoning the life out of her. With a weak smile for him and asking about his day, she hangs her coat and starts to prepare his supper.

Do I have enough money for gas? Is some dumbass going to veer off the exit ramp at the last second? Most accidents happen at intersections.

As it always does, The Memory creeps into his forethoughts. The late night at work. Feeling of exhilaration as he mounts his bike to head home. The Cadillac swerving into his path. The split second of flight as he hurtles over the handlebars. The crunching impact of the telephone pole on his back. The weeks of surgery. The endless insurance forms. The fruitless lawsuits.

She moves aside the tube into which he puffs to move his wheelchair, wiping applesauce slipping from his slack mouth. She feeds him another spoonful, and all he thinks is:

"God, I'd give anything for those carefree days again!"

***

Shock and Awww!
Not everything in space is what it seems

ATTACK

So their starship was in the process of eating our starship. A situation I do not think of fondly. We were cruising through the galaxy, minding our own business (that business being to politely subjugate non-space-faring worlds into our coalition of planets) when a crystalline ship in the shape of a giant pyramid pops out of nowhere, extends a giant tube of some sort and starts blasting away at us. Before our bridge crew could respond, the aliens sucked in some debris, and disappeared again. I only assume it was before our bridge crew could respond because I am far, far away from the bridge. As far away as my superior officer could keep me. In all honesty, I am okay with that. If I were in charge of an alien attack, I would aim for the engines, the weapons, and the bridge; not necessarily in that order. I was happy to not be in any of those places. Truth be told, given the sections of the ship that had just been vaporized, I was happy to be anywhere. But particularly not in a high-value target area.

Now, despite the fact that I think our ship is enormous, when drawing up a space-faring starship, crew quarters are the

least of the designers' considerations. I shared my quarters with
two other crewmen with bunks that folded themselves into the
walls and a single computer station. Located down the hall, the
head and shower facilities we shared with an unknown number
of other crewmen. Better than a prison cell, but only
marginally.

Over a period of days, the crystalline pyramid kept
popping in and out of existence in a new location, dissecting us
with some sort of energy weapon, sucking up the debris and
dead crew people into that giant tube, and then popping back
out of reality. They have pulled this trick several times now.
Once, eleven days earlier; again, three days after that. This
most recent attack was five days after their second pass. We
knew—and by "we," I mean the bridge crew—that they
weren't just cloaking themselves, because our tactical officer
would put a couple of missiles right where they popped away, a
half second too late. Us lowly crewmen were getting all this
third or fourth hand via a hidden channel on our neural
networks. Some enterprising engi-nerd type coded an
untraceable peer-to-peer network that fed us unofficial status
reports of the real goings-on aboard, immediately dubbed
RumorNet. The command crew turned a blind eye to this
unsanctioned channel because it saved them the effort of
keeping the crew up to date and gave them plausible deniability
for any inaccuracies and informational security breaches. Plus,
it was free and didn't cost them anything to maintain. Say what
you will about SpaceForce, but they keep an eye on the budget.

RumorNet spewed out information by the metric tonne
about the destruction areas, lives lost in the attack, and the
general status of the conflict. Even as an explosion rocked our
room and the blast disrupted life support and gravity.

*

ONE WEEK EARLIER

"So, Lewis, first posting on a starship?" the ship's doctor,
Stevenson, asked.

"My first posting ANYWHERE," I said. "I finished boot a while back and deadheaded here from Alpha Centauri 6 on the DeGrassi. It took a bit to get here, wherever here is."

"How do you like it so far?" Stevenson asked as he adjusted the sensors on the diagnostic couch.

"It's very different from boot camp. There, we had days and hours to formulate plans and make decisions. Out here, we have fractions of a second. And the technology! In boot camp, they focused on critical thinking, loyalty, and character. Basically, breaking down our individuality and personality. You know, the usual stuff. Not so much the latest techno-toys. There are things here people on Earth never imagined."

"Actually, they probably did imagine them there," Stevenson said. "We just use them out in the field. As for split-second decision making, don't worry too much about that. Our captain takes credit for all that. I want you to lay there and relax a bit. I'm going to take some of your blood and store it."

"Why?"

"In case of emergency."

"What kind of emergency?" I asked, suddenly concerned.

"One in which you would need some of your own blood, of course. While we wait, tell me a little bit about yourself. I haven't had a chance to read your file. How did you land your envious position on the *Hawking*?"

"Probably nothing you haven't heard a hundred times, Doc."

*

SIX MONTHS EARLIER

I was arrested for having sex with a minor. Now before you get all "What-a-pig!" I am not a pedophile ... or an idiot. I asked her age. I even asked her for her ID card first. It said she was twenty-two. How should I have known that the years on Alpha Centauri 6 are only nine months long? When checking her ID, I *may* have neglected, in my heightened emotional state, to notice that she had the same last name as the territorial governor. Okay, maybe I am an idiot.

The magistrate I found myself in front of, did not find "Nuh-uh!" as a legal defense. His honor gave me the choice between ten years as a guest of the territorial corrections facility, or "Tell him what's behind door number two, Johnny:" five years in the space service. I made the choice that any intelligent fellow would, I ran. When they caught me two days later, I chose ten years in the space service as opposed to three times that amount in a slightly less hospitable environment. Five extra years for two days of hiding in a bus locker seems a bit excessive. Looking ahead at my upcoming ten-year career as a crewman third class, I may have made the wrong choice.

INDUCTION

As you probably know, one of the first things they do after basic training strips away your will to live, is implant a military grade neural implant at the base of your skull. "Military grade" means "mass manufactured by the lowest bidder." The communications function theoretically may operate more securely, but it itched like the devil. They don't implant them earlier because if you die during boot camp, they would have wasted an implant.

"Is that gonna hurt?—OWWW!"

"Yes."

"You could give a fellow a little warning, you know."

"Why?"

I may have thought long and hard about the corpsman's ancestry and his relationship to his mother in those last few seconds of being off the grid. I may not have, but that's not where the smart money played.

He explained the neural network implant with all the bedside manner you would expect from a low-level military medic.

"The neural implant releases nanobytes that insert themselves into the proper areas of your cerebellum to facilitate communications, tracking, computer interfacing, and provide unique access to technology, areas of your postings, and data storage. It also tells time."

I quit listening after "nanobytes that insert themselves into the proper areas of your cerebellum." I don't remember volunteering to have microscopic machines crawling through my skull. I also don't remember the judge asking.

For the most part, when the implant works properly, it's pretty ingenious. It locks you out of doors you are not allowed to enter, keeps you from accessing the computer functions and data you shouldn't access, enables you to send and receive (what I would consider less than) "secure" communications just by thinking them a certain way, and allows the space service to track you anywhere. Anywhere. All things I am not a big proponent of. Of course, if I were in charge of a large space service that recruits a great deal of its lower ranks through the judicial process, it's exactly what I would do. Some of those people are incorrigible.

Armed with an itching spot on the back of my neck, I left the B.I.T.C.H. (Basic Induction Transition Center—quit worrying about where the H went) to report to my temporary quarters while awaiting a posting. My posting was on the *U.S.S. Hawking*, which I finally made it to three weeks later.

*

I, VACUUM

In case some other species finds this journal, I guess I should give them a heads up about us. We are basically humanoid in nature. Every school kid knows the theory that humans were "seeded," along with thousands of other worlds, from a star-spanning race long lost to history. Two arms, two legs, ten fingers, and ten toes (more unique than you might imagine among the stars), and a head that contains our faces and what our drill sergeants laughingly referred to as our brains. An endoskeleton of very breakable bone material surrounded by musculature and nerve endings contains the whole enchilada. We consider ourselves "human." And not just human, but The Humans. A perception that several thousand other systems might disagree with. Scientists believe that there are more than one hundred billion planets in the Milky Way Galaxy. And over one hundred billion galaxies.

I said all that to say this: in my humble opinion, there is only ONE Lewis Haversham III in all the universe. My drill sergeant said he was very thankful for that.

I think of myself as a survivor. Survivors do what they can to continue their basic functions in life. I've gotten used to eating ... and breathing. I'm real fond of breathing. Your species may not need to, but it's tops of my seven essential functions. Numbers three through seven include: eating, drinking, sleeping, smoking cigars, and disposing of bodily wastes. Number two should go without saying.

My new superior (do NOT call him an officer) on the *Hawking*, Sergeant M'Bari, at our first meeting, made my former drill sergeant seem warm and cuddly by comparison. He loved me. That's what I took away from our first interaction. He may have said something along the lines of "bending me over and using me like a two-credit station trollop if I got out of line." I took that as "he loved me." Our second meeting was not quite as heart-warming. I was sitting in my quarters with one of my two "roomies" about to light up a cigar when he exploded into the room. Note: Sergeants do not enter a room, they impact it. Sgt. M'Bari stands about half my height again, twice my width, and about five times my physical fitness. The man is the size of a shuttle craft.

"Son, if you light up that cigar, I'm going to arrange it so you can smoke the whole thing ... Outside."

Now I'm down to six basic functions.

On a ship with a compliment of about two hundred and forty people (I use that term species-neutral), everyone wears multiple hats. Based on my aptitude tests and Sgt. M'Bari's recommendation, I earned a fairly prestigious posting: janitorial, maintenance, security, and generally anything anyone in rank above me wants me to do. Everyone is above me in rank. All that may not sound important, but Sgt. M'Bari says "those toilets won't clean themselves!" Actually, they do, but I didn't think it prudent to correct him at that time. See the part about where I really like to breathe. I scored a prestigious security team post. "Prestigious" because if there is ever anything dangerous onboard, I am part of the elite team that is in the front lines. There was no counting my joy.

So my career as a crewman third class launched. I maintained a fairly low profile since I noticed that showing any kind of initiative may end up with you on an away mission to a sometimes hostile planet. Many of my fellow crewmen did not return from those missions. And yet, the bridge crew always did. Coincidence? I think not. There was a brief conspiracy theory about what color shirts they wore, but since all crewmen wear a bland coverall-like jumpsuit, it quickly dissipated. The current rumor is that the bridge crew uses them as human shields. No one has come back from an away mission that will disprove that story.

Security duty involves breaking up an occasional crew fight and repelling boarders. Since no one has ever boarded a SpaceForce ship, I janitor. And I try not to be exceptional at it. Who knows? Maybe there will be a need for an exceptional janitor on some away mission. I could probably live a long and happy life *without* living as an underachiever, but why take the chance?

I, with a few others, maintain the ship's robotic maintenance staff. We oversee the cleaning, painting, and upkeep. With little robotic boxes doing most of the serious work, I have a lot of downtime. It's a big ship. One could easily lose themselves on it and avoid attracting the attention of the officers quite easily. Since there are almost no crew fights, I often find downtime on one of the cots in an unused cell of the brig. It's a hard job, but someone has to do it. After all, if the bridge crew is the best and the brightest, they have to be superior to someone. I found my niche.

*

"Lewis, your personality encompasses the three C's: cowardly, cheap, and conceited." That was Mom.

First of all, Mom, I am not a coward. I think of myself as very brave. It takes a certain type of courage to not worry what other people will think when you bravely extricate yourself from situations in which you might come to physically harm.

And another thing: I am not cheap. Just six years ago, I bought you a Mother's Day gift. Granted, I bought her a ball cap at a spaceport gift shop, but I still paid real credits for it. I don't remember how I got the credits.

In addition, I do not think of myself as conceited. I believe that I am very humble despite my video star handsomeness. You're just jealous.

Fortunately, my dear old dad, during one of his more sober and lucid moments, thought more of his oldest child.

"Son, with a mind like yours, you are going to go places. Big places." I didn't know he meant the territorial corrections facility. Dad never was my biggest fan. Turns out he was right. I've been to enormous planetary systems. Well, I was in the *ship* that went to them. Except for one furlough, I haven't been off a ship in months. But the ships are pretty big. So, the old man was right on the money about me.

*

INVITATION TO EVACUATION

I was only floating for a moment when the explosive decompression blew out the bulkhead wall. As the oxygen blasted into empty space, that black maw in the hull pulled me toward it. I gripped the edge of the bunk and held on for dear life. I don't want to die. It's a big thing with me. I don't have any regrets, but if I had the chance to live my life over again ... well ... it makes me tired just thinking about it. I know it's unlikely, but it's still worth giving it a shot. I held on to the bunk as I watched one of my roommates sucked into the void. I never did learn his name. He will always be "Unnamed Roommate Number Two" to me. A fraction of a second after he fell forever into space, an invisible energy field sealed the room and automatic systems re-pressurized the area. A second too late for Unnamed Roommate Number Two, but right on time for me. With gravity restored, I fell to the flooring in a heap of tan jumpsuit and flop sweat.

Oh for those glorious moments when the beautiful Lieutenant Wa was treating me like a leper. Good times.

*

Turns out that the damage control team had more to concern themselves with than the cabin of three minor crewmen. They clearly did not place as much value on my health as I did. Holding my head, as if to nurse the universe's worst hangover, I managed to get to my feet, happy to see them still attached. The energy barrier still held in the atmosphere, but since lowest bidder manufactured that emergency field generator as well, I wanted out of that room ASAP.

As I watched the alien craft disappear from view, I concentrated on my neural implant's main communication channels, trying to contact the first response team (or anyone really), but all I could "hear" was a blast of high-pitched screaming static from the direction of the hole in my wall. I fell to the bottom bunk, the blanket and pillow long lost into space.

*

SIX HOURS EARLIER

I had spent months successfully avoiding the watchful eye of any officer on whatever ship I happened to be on and was happily trying to remain invisible. I had set up several small underground gambling operations, a bootleg porn streaming vid rental network, and a morally ambiguous massage service onboard. I narrowly avoided being caught at any of these, sometimes only just, and surprisingly earned very few extra credits. It turned out to be a lot of hard work avoiding hard work. Whoever said "crime doesn't pay" must have been following my lead. I look back at all the schemes I involved myself in over the course of my life: some were profitable and some were mine.

I was just coming back from failing to collect a debt that a crewman owed me for some interactive adult vid feeds via his neural net when I ran into the curvaceous Lt. Wa. Literally ran into her. Best part of my day. Considering the way my day turned out, that was not saying much.

Lt. Wa is also Human, but from a curious bloodline that gave her the most exotic features and a body that most lower deck crewmen only dreamed of. For some reason, she did not find it amusing that someone had nicknamed her "Lt. Wow." Whoever created that sexist pronunciation should go to the brig instead of running several small underground gambling operations, a bootleg porn vid rental network, and a morally ambiguous massage service. The bottom line was: she was very sexy. We had a lot in common.

"Excuse me, Lieutenant." Doing my best to *not* extricate my limbs from hers, after rounding a corner and bumping into her chest first.

"It's quite all right. If you would step back, that is." I could tell she was really partial to me.

"My pleasure." Who says single entendre is dead?

"Crewman, do I know you?" Trying to stay hidden from the bridge crew was now biting me in the ass.

"Haversham, ma'am ... er ... sir. Crewman Lewis Haversham III, at your service."

"Well, Crewman Lewis Haversham III, do you always accost senior officers in such a manner in the hallway?"

"No ma'am. Just the attractive ones." Wit, thy name is Lewis.

You heard it. I said she was attractive. She said I was drop dead gorgeous. Well, not exactly those words, but "drop dead" was in there somewhere.

"Don't you have duties to attend to, Crewman Lewis Haversham III? If not, I am sure some can be arranged."

"No, Lieutenant ... I mean yes, Lieutenant. I have duties to attend to." I am positively ingenious in my small talk. "Is there anything I can do to you? Uh ... for you?"

"You can step off and not accost me in the future."

"I don't want you to go away thinking I'm an idiot." I truly wanted her to think as much of me as I did.

"Why not? That's the way I started."

I backed away, knowing I had made a lasting impression. I was practically floating on air right up until the moment six hours later when I was literally floating on air.

*

RESCUED?

The damage control team did eventually rescue me. Tears of joy streamed down my face and I'm sticking to that story.

"Crewman, report to the bridge!" the sergeant in charge of damage and rescue ordered.

"Why? This is NOT my fault." That last sentence I was considering having tattooed on my forehead.

"Captain's orders. Now move."

The good news: turns out that I, specifically, had been not ordered to the bridge, but the entire security contingent had. The bad news: I *am* the entire (surviving) security team. Seems Security was having a birthday party for one of the members in the galley when a blast from the invading ship either vaporized them instantly, removed all their oxygen, or sucked them into space through the resulting hole in the bulkhead. It seems outrageously unfair. They didn't invite me.

*

The scene on the bridge was a singular voice of chaos. The captain was barking orders. Everyone else was staring off into space, communicating via their implants, totally ignoring him.

"Lt. Wa! Report!" the captain snapped out.

"So far, we have fifteen casualties or unaccounted for, six injured, two of those critically. Dr. Stephenson has co-opted a xeno-botanist and a cook, both with medical cross training as assistants. Repairs are commencing on all affected decks. Environmental fields are holding until permanent hull plating can be replaced."

"What is happening with our friends out there?" the captain asked.

"The attack has subsided," Lt. Wa reported. "We were unable to effectively counter-attack so the decision to retreat was entirely theirs. We have no idea how they are able to phase in and out of normal space so readily. However they do it, leaves no energy signature behind. Our best guess: they have headed toward the closest system."

"What is our engine status?" the captain asked.

"Slider Drive is still viable, but not recommended with huge portions of the hull missing," Lt. Wa said.

"Yeah, well I don't recommend getting sliced and diced by a crystal pyramid, but we don't always get what we want. Lieutenant Davis, set course for that system at flank speed," the captain ordered the navigator/pilot. "What's our ETA for that system?

"At top speed, sir," Davis stated, "about twelve days."

"Twelve days?" I blurted out before thinking. I do that a lot. "I thought the ship's Slider Drive was faster than light. Why does it take so long? That system is right there."

"Who is this idiot?" the captain barked.

"Crewman Lewis Haversham III. Currently our entire security detachment," Lt. Wa said cooly.

"We are so screwed," the captain said under his breath. "Well, Crewman, the reason it will take so long to travel such a relatively short distance is: it will take the computer four days to calculate our jump to faster than lightspeed, unless of course you would like to try it without exact calculations. It will take four days for us to gradually work our way up to that speed, unless you would like to be smashed to a jelly-like goo on the back bulkheads by the G-forces. From there, we travel a few hours at supra-lightspeed. Then it will take us four days to slow to a survivable speed, unless you would like to be smashed into a jelly-like goo on the forward bulkheads. So twelve days is not so bad for a three quarters of a light-year trip, wouldn't you say?"

"No, sir," I stammered. "I always prefer the goo-free option."

"Lt. Wa, tell the engineering team they have four days to get this bucket ship shape. I want us battle ready by the time we hit that system. And get that ... guy (indicating the entirety of the security team whose name he didn't bother to remember) and whoever else you can round up down to the SLIP room and get them up to speed as quickly as possible."

Lt. Wow grabbed me by the arm and dragged me out the door of the bridge. We met Sgt. M'Bari heading for the bridge.

"M'Bari, you're with us," she ordered.

With a single "hmph," he did an about-face and followed us to the SLIP chamber. I'm sure he was scowling at the back of my head the whole way. Turns out I was not the only member of the security team left alive. He didn't make the birthday party invitation list either.

"Lieutenant? I'm not being purposefully dense, but what is a SLIP?" I asked.

"Good thing it's not on purpose."

*

TECHNICAL SPECS FOR DUMMIES

Turns out SLIP stands for "Solid Light Image Projection." Quite brilliant, actually. It was meant for away parties to do planetary exploration without having to leave the safety of the ship.

We fire a SLIP missile down to the planet. It pops open and ejects SLIP backpacks. Solid light holograms of crew members who remotely "pilot" them from casket-like pods onboard. They are actually manipulating human shaped force fields with holograms projected over top of them to give themselves the appearance they would normally have. That's for psychological and ease of use reasons. They could program it so you would look like an Antarean, but who would want to? Except Antareans, I mean. The hologram forcefields wear devices on their holographic backs to maintain their density and communicate with each other and the ship. The landing party doesn't have to worry about atmosphere, bio-hazards, or radiation. They control their holograms and communicate with each other through "quantum comms" which seems to me like telepathy, but let the engi-nerds explain the science. Distance is not an issue for quantum comms which also transmits and records 3D images and data back to ship.

"We may not have time for a proper training session," Lt. Wa said. "You'll just have to learn very quickly. On-the-job training as it were."

"Hey! There's no call for that sort of language," I protested. "Learn" and "job" are two of my least favorite words. Also not a big fan of "responsible," "earn," and "volunteer."

"Get in the pod," Sgt. M'Bari growled.

*

ON THE JOB TRAINING

Sgt. M'Bari did not get into a pod as he had plenty of experience piloting a SLIP. Instead, he joined the two technicians who monitored our life signs and data flow. An important job because if you die in a pod, you're ... you know ... dead. While we waited for the SLIP missile to launch, the technicians scanned us for stress factors.

"Crewman Haversham, while your SLIP personae cannot be harmed during the exploration, your physical body, here, can be impacted by an unforeseen event. This is one of the reasons we do not allow anyone with a cardiac history to pilot SLIPs," the technician explained. "Under adverse conditions, it harms the driver."

What could be stressful about facing off with alien warriors? I'm just a janitor. How did I get into this mess?

"But it's safe, right?" I said while attempting to climb back out of the pod.

"Oh yes. We almost never lose anyone."

"Almost?" I said, as he gently pushed me back into the pod with a smile on his face.

"Those hardly count. Just ask the bridge crew."

"Relax, Haversham," I heard Lt. Wow say inside my head. "You're as safe here as your mother's womb."

"What if Mom was an alcoholic, drugged-out, suicidal cliff-diver?"

"Then you're safer here."

"Just lay back and relax," the technician said. "Clear your head of all thoughts."

"Shouldn't be a problem for him," Sgt. M'Bari transmitted.

*

It took them few minutes to target a nearby largish asteroid and fire the SLIP missile at it. Lt. Wow and I laid together quietly. Well, in separate pods with several technicians and Sgt. M'Bari standing over us. It could have been more romantic. The missile must have ejected our backpacks properly because the next thing I know, I am standing on the surface of the asteroid with Lt. Wow giving me instruction in piloting the SLIP.

"As you can see, the image looks just like you. Unfortunately. With more time, we can program it to project a more physically fit, more handsome, version of you. It doesn't change your holograms ability, but it's psychologically more effective."

"You mean I perform better if I look better?" I asked.

"No, it makes me less nauseous," Lt. Wa said with a straight face. I looked at her holographic avatar. It looked very much like her. Dark hair, tied in a SpaceForce-approved ponytail. Lean body with ample curves. Her eyes, lips, and cheekbones in competition for Most Exotic Feature. Either she didn't feel the need to enhance her holographic image or I always see her in an optimized form in my mind. It was weird seeing her in her somewhat form-fitting tan uniform, with just a slim backpack and no space suit, considering we were standing on an asteroid hurtling through the vacuum of space.

"Just move as you always do," Lt. Wa continued with her training lecture. "The computer onboard translates your synaptic impulses to the SLIP at quantum speed so there is no noticeable lag. The force field skinning your hologram enables you to interact with physical objects. You cannot reduce your image's density or the backpack would have nothing to hang on to. It would also screw up the computer that allows us to simulate gravity in this form."

"There's gravity here?"

"No. The computer and backpacks just simulate it to make it easier for you to navigate. With a few mental commands through your neural interface, you can adjust your strength, stamina, and various physical reactions to have your holograph perform amazing feats. I don't recommend it while in training. It's hard enough teaching you how to walk without falling, let alone leaping ten stories."

"So most new trainees have a hard time just walking in their SLIP units?" I asked.

"No, I am just banking on your usual coordination and intelligence," Lt. Wa said.

"The SLIP fields are impervious to physical damage, but I don't recommend testing that theory as your backpack is not. You aren't really here or breathing, so a hostile atmosphere or biological agents such as viruses or diseases are no problem," Lt. Wa continued. "There are a few limitations. While the sensors in the backpacks record and transmit gaseous chemical data, the holograms have no sense of smell. On some of the planets I have been to, that would be a blessing." I think that may have been her first attempt at humor. Ever.

"The SLIPs also can't carry any weapons," she explained as we jogged across the surface of the asteroid. "No need to defend ourselves since these are just force fields covered in holograms. We normally just use these exploring new worlds. SLIPs can't project beams like energy weapons."

Oh, come on now! We are talking about the possibility of encountering a hostile force, a blaster wouldn't suck, hologram or no hologram. Did no one think about strapping one onto a backpack before loading the missile?

After about three hours of running, scanning, and throwing bigger and bigger rocks, I transmitted to Lt. Wa: "If I'm just a hologram, why do I feel so thirsty?"

"That's your real body. You have a bit of cotton mouth and may be a little dehydrated. One more lesson and we will take a break," the lieutenant said. "Epsilon."

"What's 'epsilon'?" I asked. Turns out she was transmitting to M'Bari.

Right where the lieutenant was standing, a gigantic creature of rock, scales, and teeth appeared, snarling at its next potential meal.

I looked around for the lieutenant, and not finding her, followed my instincts. I ran. I was nearly a half a kilometer away when I realized that I was a hologram and the creature couldn't really hurt me. I also realized the lieutenant hadn't followed my very intelligent lead. I turned, ran back to the beast, and in my most arrogant stance, flipped it the bird. "WHERE'S LT. WA?"

The gigantic hand-like fist seemed to move in slow motion as it backhanded me into a boulder. As my eyelids fluttered and I blacked out, I noticed the backpack on the shoulders of the monster. And here I thought she was starting to like me.

*

EPIPHANY

"He's going into shock!" the engi-nerd shrieked. I couldn't see him, but even through the darkness around me, I could hear him. Barely.

"Leave him in the pod, but get his feet up."

"Wrap this stimulator blanket around him."

"Get an IV started and let's get some fluids in him."

"Slap that cardiac regulator on his chest."

"It's always the newbies."

An hour later, they lifted me from the SLIP pod. Even Sgt. M'Bari was gentler. Well, by his standards anyway.

"I swear I slowed that punch down. Why didn't he accelerate his SLIP and evade?" Lt. Wa was asking no one in general.

"The little idiot probably didn't know you could do that." Sgt. M'Bari's gravel-like voice.

"The 'little idiot' is right here, and NO, I didn't know you could do that," I croaked.

"You mean, you came back for me, thinking that Andromedan Rock Beast had me, and you didn't know you could accelerate your speed?" Lt. Wa asked in amazement.

"Yeah."

"That ... that ... that is the ... dumbest thing I have ever heard in my life!" Lt. Wa snarled. "The smart move would have been to realize you could dodge the blow. No. Scratch that. The smart move would have been to run away as fast as you could and protect your SLIP."

"I thought it as incredibly brave."

"You *thinking* is highly unlikely. You managed to destroy a very expensive piece of equipment," the lieutenant said. Then in a quieter voice, "And you could have been killed, you moron."

"So, not brave?"

"Not smart," she said a little more gently.

We sat there in silence. The SLIP engi-nerd fussed over my readings and IV. Lt. Wa fumed. Sgt. M'Bari grinned. And me ... I had an epiphany.

It's not that the bridge officers use the crew as human shields during away missions, it's that the crew doesn't have enough experience in the SLIPs and get themselves killed. Wait till this hits the RumorNet. It's possible to survive an away mission. I am living proof.

"I wanna go back!"

The engi-nerd was the first to regain his voice. "Are you insane? You just barely survived *that* attempt."

"The more SLIP missions I survive, the more likely I will survive a SLIP mission." I swear it made more sense when I said it in my head.

Sgt. M'Bari raised an eyebrow. Lt. Wa just stared at me as if I had grown another head. Maybe I had.

The technician insisted that we eat, had plenty to drink, and a quick nap before we returned to SLIP pods. This time Sgt. M'Bari accompanied us to the asteroid. There were plenty of SLIPs to allow him to do so, I just think he wanted to see it to believe it. I insisted that he and Lt. Wa give me advanced SLIP training. Mental note: Do *not* insist on anything ever again.

*

CHANGE IN PLANS

Nearly four days later, we stepped back on to the bridge together. This marked my first time back since starting SLIPs training.

"Lt. Davis, prepare to initiate Slider Drive," the captain ordered.

"Sir. If I may. I think we should wait," Lt. Wa interjected.

"Why in the universe should we do that, Lieutenant?" the captain growled.

"Sir, while we were in SLIPs training, I was wondering why the aliens didn't attack us again."

She had time to think about *that* while I was fighting for my life against her and M'Bari's holographic horrors?

"Go on."

"I think we could save considerable energy just waiting for them to come to us. They only seem to be attacking on prime number days. I checked some historical records and a few centuries ago, there were some reports of a similar incident back on Earth that confirms that theory. If I'm right," the lieutenant continued, "we will only have to wait seven more days."

"So, we just wait around for them to destroy us? Is that your plan, Lieutenant?" the captain said, somewhat less than convinced. "Just *exactly* how did they defeat them once upon a time?"

"Trickery, sir," Lt. Wa said.

Then I did something that surprised everyone. No one moreso than I.

"I might have an idea about that sir."

"The idiot speaks," the captain said, clearly enamored with me.

"Sir, it may be worth listening to Lewi ... Crewman Haversham, he has some experience with ... deceit," Lt. Wa added. She had taken the time to look up my record. I was touched.

"Hmph." I'm not sure, but I think that was Sgt. M'Bari agreeing.

"All right, Haversham, what is this plan?"

"Sir, have you ever heard of Three Card Monte?"

It took me the better part of an hour to explain what I had in mind. It actually would have been less, but Lt. Wa and even Sgt. M'Bari kept interjecting tactical suggestions. Okay, maybe they *did* improve the plan. It wasn't so much a plan really. More of an idea. At the end of it, I wasn't being ordered into an airlock, an upgrade from my usual schemes.

"This is potentially the dumbest thing I have ever heard."

Tell us how you really feel, Captain.

"Sir, with all due respect," Lt. Wa said, "do we have another plan?"

The captain mulled that over for a second or two.

"Fine. What are you waiting for? This dumbass plan won't do it itself."

Lt. Wa, after a glance at me, fairly ran away. Toward the SLIPs lab. Sgt. M'Bari barrelled toward the armory. Lt. Davis immediately crawled under the control panels for the communication and sensor arrays.

I spent some time on the RumorNet with the crew, then headed to sickbay.

It took me several minutes of arguing with Dr. Stephenson to get him to part with his beloved hemoglobin reserves, but I finally found the right logic.

"If this doesn't work, we won't need them anyway." Hardly an encouraging argument, but effective.

*

Seven days later, we were as ready as we could be in that amount of time. I stood on the bridge brimming with false confidence, secure in the knowledge that similar to what I had told the doctor, if this didn't work, I would never see the court martial coming.

*

RUN SILENT, RUN MONTE

True to Lt. Wa's calculations, exactly eleven days after the last attack, the crystalline pyramid appeared in space, tube extended to resume its duties.

Our ship listed in space, seemingly dead, with tons of debris floating around it. And lots of bio matter.

The pyramid did not expect that.

A half dozen pieces of debris blinked from sight.

Without warning, seventy-two starships, appeared in space, all aimed in the direction of the pyramid.

The pyramid did not expect that either.

One second later, the ships disappeared and reappeared in a different position.

Yep, you guessed it: The pyramid did not expect that. It was a day of surprises for them.

Seconds later, miraculously, the pyramid exploded from the inside.

Even more miraculously, I was still alive to watch it. Though part of me wished for a quick, clean death.

*

BEHIND THE SCENES

I know you are dying to know how I did this. Well, I didn't. Everyone did. It was just my ingenious idea that inspired our survival and the total annihilation of our enemies. In my humble opinion.

The lovely Lt. Wa wrangled the engi-nerds to program a dozen SLIP missiles to eject a half dozen backpacks as usual, except now, each which would generate holograms of SpaceForce ships on a signaled command. Tons of debris from earlier run-ins collected by the crew, which yours truly coordinated via RumorNet, deposited the wreckage into the airlocks, along with the SLIP missiles. The blown-out debris also contained large quantities of bio matter thanks to Dr. Stephenson's blood banks and the few remaining bodies left on board after the first attacks.

We knew approximately where the alien vessel would appear thanks to Lt. Davis configuring the communications and sensor arrays to detect the static the pyramids generate when phasing. The computer used that data to aim all the holographic ships generally in that direction.

Sgt. M'Bari only had time to re-engineer six missiles with tactical warheads, near-lightspeed power plants, and instantaneous and automatic guidance for the tube openings. He is *such* a slacker.

The nanosecond the pyramid arrived, the six warheads took advantage of the aliens' shock of both seeing us incapacitated and then finding themselves surrounded by SpaceForce ships. Being unmanned, the missiles didn't have to worry about G-forces turning anyone into goo. Their speed was almost instantaneous and they seemed to blink out of sight, traveling at near-lightspeed into the tube.

As soon as the warheads disappeared, our ship took off at its highest sub-lightspeed on a random course, zigzagging away from the blast area. The timing and coordination of all this was so critical that the preprogramed computer executed it. That includes the sudden course changes, which as much as it shames me to say, enabled me to repaint a corner of the bridge with motion sickness.

*

AFTERMATH

"Good job, every—WHAT IS THAT SMELL?" the captain bellowed, turning in my direction.

"My stomach may not have reacted as well as it could have during the sudden course corrections," I said weakly.

Lt. Davis snickered, Sgt. M'Bari provided "Hmph."

"Be that as it may, your plan seemed to work, Ensign Haversham," the captain said.

"*Ensign* Haversham?" I asked, somewhat surprised.

"What's the point of being captain if I can't give battlefield commissions?"

"But—"

"Lt. Wa will supervise your officer training, upgrade your implant, and as soon as she thinks you're able, you will assume your duties as tactical and security chief."

"Thank you, sir," unable to keep the shock from my voice. Then it hit me. "Does that mean I would be Sgt. M'Bari's supervising officer?"

"I guess it would."

"Hmph." That was me.

Lt. Wa smiled. Sgt. M'Bari did not.

***

ABOUT THE AUTHOR

Paul K. Metheney

Paul was the featured author for dozens of sports magazine articles, has numerous stories published in various Left Hand Publishers and independent anthologies (*Beautiful Lies, Painful Truths Vol.1, Beautiful Lies, Painful Truths Vol.2, It's About Time, Classics ReMixed Vol. I,* and *Classics ReMixed Vol. II*), and is working on a much-delayed novel or two.

Paul has nearly three decades working in advertising design, print, and graphic design. For nearly thirty years or so, he has been working in the web design, SEO, PPC, social media, and marketing fields, including writing marketing copy for his clients' blogs and social media.

Paul is happily married to his one-time high school sweetheart, loves riding his Can-Am Spyder motorcycle, occasionally smokes a good cigar, and is an avid poker enthusiast. Paul, his wife, and two dogs are currently living full-time in an RV, traveling the country.

Paul can be reached at his blog on writing, poker, travel, reviews, and all things politically incorrect at paulmetheney.com, on Twitter at http://Twitter.com/PaulMetheney, and on Facebook at http://facebook.com/Paul.Metheney.

The title of the book derives from a strip bar bouncer in the '80s taking one look at Paul and saying

"That boy ain't right in the head."

More from Paul K. Metheney

Books where you can find books, short stories, and collections by the author.

Concepts for Texas Hold'em
By Paul K. Metheney

PLAY FOR PAY!

An easy-to-read pocket guide of concepts, notes, thoughts, and strategies on making more money at the Texas Hold'em Poker tables in casinos. From tactics to use at the table, to money management, to etiquette & terminology, Concepts for Texas Hold'em will steer you toward bigger profits from your poker sessions. Aimed at intermediate to advanced players, we skip over the basics of the game to tricks, tips, and thoughts on how to make the most from your play.

Maximize your wins in your casino cash games of Texas Hold'em Poker. Minimize your losses.
Learn from the superstars.

***

That Boy Ain't Write in the Head
By Paul K. Metheney

A Collection of Mixed Genre Stories: Sci-Fi, Alternate Universes, Time Travel, Supernatural, & More

A science-fiction author tries to save the world from alien attack, siblings must learn to adjust to the brother's newfound powers, alien visitors that only eat cancer, a man travels back to his past, and a Secret Service agent must protect his friend, the President, from destroying the White House. These are just a few of the new and fantastic tales that await you inside.

From sci-fi to stark reality, these short stories will entertain, provoke, and whet your appetite for more. This collection contains not only serves up the best of Paul K. Metheney's short stories, but an all new menu of fresh tales to stimulate your literary palate.

Posse Whipped
By Paul K. Metheney

A Southern sheriff struggles to save his town from corruption, drug-trafficking, moonshiners, and the economy, all while protecting his most valuable law-enforcement assets ... his family and friends. As the sheriff protects his town and family, a villain from his family's past assembles his own eclectic posse of criminals to destroy Sheriff MacDowell and everything he holds dear.

A down-home journey into the hills of Kentucky, as author, Paul K. Metheney, brings you a sometimes humorous novel set in a modern day western fight for survival, justice, and family. The spirit of the Wild West meets modern day in an adventure for the John Wayne in us all.

"If you like Craig Johnson's *Walt Longmire Mysteries*, you will LOVE *Posse Whipped*."

"All of C.J. Box's action, but with Metheney's humor and wit."

***

Two Minds, No Waiting
By Steve Rouse & Paul K. Metheney

Take two very disturbed minds. Add the ability to create any worlds or situations they like. And you have the recipe for a collection of science fiction stories like none you have ever tasted.

From alien saviors and attackers, to time travel, to fantastic tales that include unique teachers and hunted mammals. More than just spaceships and phaser beams, this collection contains alternate universes and superheroes. If you're ready to set aside your beliefs in what is or isn't possible, it's time to get your imagination rewired by ...

Two Minds, No Waiting!

LHP Web Site - https://bit.ly/2KOnfi7
Amazon - https://amzn.to/39jAjFm

***

Classics Remixed Vol. I

An anthology of short stories twisting classic stories and your imagination in all new ways.

Alternate versions of stories you know taking you in new directions.

From much-loved fairy fables to time-honored tales, no genre or classic is off-limits. Classics ReMixed Vol. I spins and twists divergent versions of old favorites and stories we all know. Be prepared to have all your ...

Classics ReMixed

LHP Web Site - https://bit.ly/2XLgkY9
Amazon - https://amzn.to/2M0qRLx
Goodreads - https://bit.ly/2LZsIQI

***

Classics Remixed Vol. II

Continuing the anthology of short stories twisting classic stories and your imagination in all new ways.

From much-loved fairy fables to time-honored tales, no genre or classic is off limits. Classics ReMixed Vol. II spins and twists divergent versions of old favorites and stories we all know. Be prepared to have all your ...

Classics ReMixed again

LHP Web Site - https://bit.ly/2IyQGzH
Amazon - https://amzn.to/3aC5aeh
Goodreads - https://bit.ly/2vMBMDm

***

Beautiful Lies, Painful Truths Vol. I

There's an ironic beauty between humanity's love of Life and fear of Death. Life seemingly brings joy, happiness, hope, and love. Death can end sadness, illness, suffering, and pain. We asked writers to "Let the title and quote take your imagination, your story, wherever it wants to go."

Join them now as an international blend of authors, both fresh and seasoned, bring you an exceptional menu of speculative fiction, mystery, realism, horror, and the supernatural. If your palate varies from the macabre to the dramatic, *Beautiful Lies, Painful Truths* provides an assortment of tasty treasures that will chill, delight, and give you food for thought.

Amazon - http://amzn.to/2reSyIe
YouTube - https://youtu.be/4m1BR6BIBTM
The Reviews on YouTube -
https://youtu.be/tTtdf0LQC7Q
LHP's Web Site - http://bit.ly/2FHXzw9

***

Beautiful Lies, Painful Truths Vol. II

Most believe that Life promises light, bliss, and wonder. Death scares most with its shadow of mortality, darkness, and destruction. But what if those may be, if not lies, just facets of the complicated entities that bookend our existence? Life does not mock Death, but feeds it. Death is not the cessation of Life, but an alteration of existence. What would you do if faced with either truth?

An international galley of authors brings us a second repast of tales featuring the complex relationship between Life, Death, and humanity. From the supernatural to the sublime, these writers, both novitiates and accomplished, serve up a banquet of speculative fiction across a wide spectrum of genres.

Amazon - http://amzn.to/2ngBq0i
LHP's Web Site - http://bit.ly/2Dxu9n8
Goodreads: http://bit.ly/2slkBpP

***